FOOLS
OF A
PRIVILEGED
KIND

FOOLS OF A PRIVILEGED KIND

MR. B

XULON PRESS

Xulon Press
555 Winderley Pl, Suite 225
Maitland, FL 32751
407.339.4217
www.xulonpress.com

© 2025 by Mr. B

All rights reserved solely by the author. The author guarantees all contents are original and do not infringe upon the legal rights of any other person or work. No part of this book may be reproduced in any form without the permission of the author.

Due to the changing nature of the Internet, if there are any web addresses, links, or URLs included in this manuscript, these may have been altered and may no longer be accessible. The views and opinions shared in this book belong solely to the author and do not necessarily reflect those of the publisher. The publisher therefore disclaims responsibility for the views or opinions expressed within the work.

Paperback ISBN-13: 979-8-86850-996-4
Ebook ISBN-13: 979-8-86850-997-1

"FOOLS OF A PRIVILEGED KIND"

The official recorded time was 2:13 A.M. in a call on the first Saturday in July to the Stanislaus 911 number by Eddie Duvalle, a homeless transient living at the time on McHenry Avenue in Modesto California. In his call, Eddie gave his name, age of 43, and his status as a homeless veteran and, as he reported, something came down out of the sky like the proverbial thief in the night, with a gust of wind that whipped up the summer's July dust that filled the air with dirt and street trash that almost tore his blanket away where he was sleeping next to a street light power box. Eddie reported that after the gust of wind, he really couldn't see what it was exactly, but it was huge, blocking out the night sky in every direction with an eerie reflection of the lights from the streets and home and businesses below that seemed to turn the world upside down. The 911 operator asked how much he had been drinking. Eddie told her he had just finished his second "40". She advised him to sleep it off.

However, just minutes later, Subsequent calls from Modesto Police and the Stanislaus Sheriff's Department street patrols lent a reality to Eddie's first report. It was, they reported, "something" extraordinarily huge that was suspended in the sky over McHenry Avenue for at least, as far as they could assess, at least two miles the length of McHenry Avenue with a width of at least a mile. No estimate as to how far up it went was given until a Medi-flight coming in from Manteca called in and reported it would have to go up twenty-five hundred feet to pass over it or go around it to get their patient to the hospital. 911 recommended it go around if it didn't jeopardize the patient's life. Later, by only minutes, estimates by the Sheriff's copter allowed that the object's depth or thickness was at least a thousand to twelve hundred feet with an absolutely smooth and unbroken surface on the sides. It looked, according to the sheriff's copter, like an incredibly huge, shiny, black domino that had a dull glow all of its own.

At three twenty-two A.M that same morning, the CNN "alert phone" by Carolyn Rush's bed jarred her wake. Still groggy from attending the retirement party for the senior West Coast correspondent George Medina whom she was replacing, Carolyn came through as the professional she was. Rubbing her eyes and clearing her throat, her response was a crisp, "Yes?" but it was then as she listened to the voice on the phone excitedly relaying information, that her mouth fell open in disbelief at what was being reported. She began to stammer. "Susan! Susan! ..Are you...are you talking about a friggin' spaceship over Modesto!?"

"Yes! Yes!" Susan confirmed, still excited. "My God! You should see it, Carolyn! Even on our phones it's unbelievable! It's huge! We've dispatched a car to pick you up. It should be at your place in about twenty minutes. Irving Becker and Malcom Carnes are already on their way to the airport. They should be ready to go when you get there. Hey...turn your phone on to our channel and take a look! Again, it's absolutely unbelievable, Carolyn!"

As Carolyn hurriedly dressed and checked her prepacked suitcase for anything else she might want to take, she stopped and thought of anything else she might need. Having Irv and Mac infused her with confidence. Irv was the best cameraman on the west coast, maybe even the best in all of CNN's stable. His sense of importance of light and angles was instinctive which was why he earned last year's CNN's best overall photographer for CNN. And Mac Carnes was always her choice for a consummate helicopter pilot. Thirty-two and military trained in the Air Force, he was a lean, buffed physical specimen of the first order. He and Irving lived together in an apartment in San Franciso and quietly cruised the gay scene. Together, at work, they were an unbeatable combination of skill and courage, and humor. And, on the gay scene, they were admired and sought after by those who did not recognize or believe their devotion to one another. For them, she pulled six cold cans of Kern Peach Nectar from the refrigerator and slipped them into an insulated bag. It was a small gesture, but it was like the ones in the past she knew had endeared them to her in their relationship. Over the years, learning of the hardship in their lives, Carolyn had come to love them as much as her own two sons who now were fortunately were away in New York spending the summer with their estranged step-father, Merl Atwood, an investment counselor who always seemed to need Carolyn's inheritance from her first husband, Clayton Rush II. Her first husband had been, like his father, a very successful investment banker himself. He had inherited an extremely successful investment company from his father, Clayton Rush Sr, and then had died of a cerebral hemorrhage after falling from one of his favorite jumping horses at the age of forty two. His sons were just two and four years old and Carolyn Rush kept his name rather than the name of her second husband whom she married three years later on the rebound, a move she soon regretted for a number of reasons.

Those thoughts were in her mind, flitting about even thought It was still dark at four thirty as Mac piloted the chopper over the hills east of Livermore and east towards Tracy, a glowing island of light surrounded by an immense darkness that was the great expanse of the central California valley. Like the perimeter of a galaxy, only a few lights pierced the great dark sea dissected by feint lines of the lights from the few early cars traveling on the I-5 freeway going north and south and the more heavily traveled Highway 120 going east to west, back toward the Bay Area and west toward Modesto which was still just a dim glow on the horizon. The steady drone of the copter's engines crushed any silence as Carolyn opened the insulated bag and pulled out two cans of still cold Kern Peach Nectar and handed one to Irv and the other to Mac. In the growling noise of the copter's engines, Carolyn couldn't hear the pop of the lids, even hers, but she raised her can and reached over to touch their cans, "Hey, here's to it's death!" She called out to her companions.

"The death of what?" Irv asked, almost shouting. "the spaceship?"

"No! To weather balloons." Carolyn laughed and her two companions burst out laughing with her.

"Yeah! What's the government going to do now?! No more balloons, no more clouds and freaky weather...or mass hallucinations." Irv added.

"...and no more keeping our mouths shut!!" Mac yelled, smiling. "You have to wonder what they're going to come up with. And if they ask me, I'm going to tell them the same old truth. I didn't see nothing!"

Irving and Carolyn laughed with Caroly nodding at his joke. "Well, they just might try telling the truth for once. But that's something I'll have to see! Hey, what are those lights over there?" She asked, pointing to a large swath spreading out slightly over to her right.

"Oh those? Those are just weather balloons." Mac smirked. "Manteca weather balloons...and those over there way beyond those... the smaller one is Ripon and the larger ones...further out there... those are Modesto weather balloons...official explanation from a good old American pilot who doesn't want to lose his license!"

Carolyn and Irv laughed again and then she squinted. "I can't see any spaceship.... can you?"

"Nope. Not yet anyway." Mac replied...but get ready for when we do."

Mr. B

Although the coming dawn was due around five o clock, it was still just a subtle glow to the East in front of them. But now that they had passed Manteca and Ripon and were closer to Modesto, it was not hard to see it, even in the darkness of the early morning hours at four thirty. It looked like a huge dark rectangle that appeared more like a power outage than anything else until Mac brought the chopper down and they could see lights glowing under the huge mass where police and sheriff patrol cars scurried in the streets, lights flashing but sirens not audible in the growl of their copters engine. Irv dutifully started recording everything, even the sudden appearance of the Channel 3 Helicopter from Sacramento. It was followed by a Stanislaus Sheriff's copter that seemed to be trying to keep them at a distance from the spaceship.

Carolyn shook her head. "Ignore them, Mac. You go where I tell you...just like always."

"And where is that?"

"Up...up on top.

"...to?"

"Land."

"What!?"

"Hey...if we can...only if we can...and let's go see now...because I don't think it's gonna be long before we're all going to be kicked out of here."

With a quick consenting nod, Mac didn't hesitate. Everyone felt the surge of power as Mac lifted the copter up alongside the space ship, watching and recording their reflection in the gleaming, polished side of the craft until it crested and then then glided over the top until Carolyn told Mac to stop and land about a hundred feet from the edge.

"What!? Are you kidding me? Are you going to get out? Carolyn?"

"Mac...Mac.. You don't have to land...just get me a foot or so above the surface so I can jump out...and Irv can follow me unless I sink up to my waist...because, damn, it looks almost wet , doesn't it? You ready, Irv?"

Carolyn opened the door and felt the summer's hot night air sweep in around her as she stepped out onto the landing rail, waiting for Mac to bring the craft down to about a foot. Carolyn looked at Irv, shot him a grimacing smile, and then jumped the foot or so. Feeling the hard surface beneath her feet, she pumped her fist in the air and let out a yell of victory into her microphone in her other hand. "Yes! Yes! Yes!" She called out to the gods in the night air above her. She held out her hand to Irv. "Hey, Irv...you remember this? 'This is one small step for man'...RIght?...Well this is one small step for a woman... and you too, Irv..but one giant leap for women!" She motioned for Mac to cut his engines and to join theml. "Come on, Mac...shut her down and join us." Then, she stomped her foot on the surface and said, "Are you listening down there? Come on out and let's talk about why you're here.! And Irv, get a picture of the three of us and send everything back to the office...and record it too. This isn't just big or huge, it's humongous! They just can't call this a spaceship...just look at it...it's a 'space-place'."

Irv laughed and dutifully followed the instructions and then gave Carolyn a bit of a questioning look as a Sheriff's copter zoomed in and the pilot and the uniformed officer waved for them to leave as Mac stepped out to join Irv and Carolyn who dutifully waved her willingness to comply with an 'OK' sign and then, in a shout over the sheriffs copter engine to Irv and Mac, she declared, "You know damn well they wish the had the huevos to do this too!...and look around...not a single 'no parking" sign! They're making it up as they go along just like we are."

A half an hour later, Mac landed at Modesto Airport and secured the craft with Irv while Carolyn rented a car to get to the tallest hotel in Modesto. At the hotel, Carolyn rented two rooms on the top floor facing north and the southern end of the 'spaceplace' and then, with Irv returning after picking up Mac, they reviewed the footage they had sent back to the office. Extremely pleased at what they had accomplished and the accolades the office was passing back to them when they finished, she urged them to get some sleep while she stared out her window at the now very clear and visible south end of the 'spaceplace". It did look like a giant domino but beyond its appearance, beyond its size, she could feel her heart pumping inside her breast as the excitement of the unknown now looming in the sky out her window would not go away. She decided then to try and reach her sons back in New York as she hoped they were, like almost all of the rest of the world, now tuned in to this phenomenal once in a lifetime experience. The phone continued to ring...she made a face. The phone kept ringing and then transferred to "leave a message", An odd thought popped into her head, she wondered if the natives in Central America had felt the same way she was feeling now when they saw the first European explorers in what to them looked like giant canoes. But, she told herself, this was far, far beyond a giant canoe. She left her message with a "Hope you've now have seen why I'm calling. Don't worry...we're all fine! Love and God Bless! Mom!" Carolyn dialed Irv's number and waited the few seconds it took for him to answer. "Hey, Love, are you still filming?"

"Oh yeah."

"Good, keep on it because I've got a feeling something is gonna pop real quick. I know you're tired but hang in there."

"Will do."

Caroyn moved a chair to where she could see the "space place", her own giant canoe, hanging absolutely motionless in the sky out her window and framed by an increasingly blue morning sky. For a few minutes she just watched, her blue eyes trying to pick out some tiny movement but there was nothing in the early morning light except suddenly, quite suddenly more helicopters, at first just a few and then like a mosquito swarm, fast and menacing, their guns facing the ship. Then, a few moments later, came the rumbling and roaring sounds of a jet so loud it shook the hotel windows. She got up and looked out to see a sleek delta winged jet flash by, higher than the copters, followed by two more. Looking further up into the bright morning sky, Carolyn saw the more distant and more menacing bombers circling like the fabled old Indians around a wagon train. She counted four of them. She sucked in a deep breath and, for the first time, felt a genuine sense of fear that was interrupted by the brash ring of her CNN phone. She snatched it up from the tabletop.

"Carolyn here." Her voice was crisp and professional, hiding her growing wariness.

"Carolyn? Sue here. Big news! President Pollard has just declared a national state of emergency. He's closed all of our borders and declared martial law for all the counties bordering Stanislaus. I've never seen things happen so fast! They've called an emergency session for the UN for tomorrow and already Russia, China, North Korea and Iran are demanding access to the spaceship. And North Korea has declared if it's denied access, they will target it with a nuclear ICBM as it's either an American ruse or a national and international threat to the North Korean Democratic Peoples Republic. They've given Pollard three days to respond. And get this. Someone leaked Pollard's private response to Korea's threat...he said to tell them that if they send a missile, we'll send twenty. Looks like things are heating up fast." When Carolyn didn't immediately respond, Sue's voice became alarmed. "Carolyn?"

"Yes, Sue... I'm here. I was just wondering if anyone has considered why it's even here...especially in Modesto. I mean what's here! Nothing really. Maybe it just broke down and it had to stop somewhere. An emergency road stop..."

Sue managed a quick laugh. "Wouldn't that be something? ...Or maybe they just want to pick up a couple tons of almonds?"

Carolyn snickered. She enjoyed Sue's humor and confidence "Right...I mean we don't know diddly right now. We're such friggin' fools when you really stop to think about it. Hey, I'm going to work on my on-sight monologue and, when Irv is through, I'll send it to you…and I'll make sure you asked if maybe all they want is a couple of tons of almonds or maybe to plug a leak in their radiator…sound good?"

Sue chuckled. "When do you think you'll have it?"

"Gimme at least an hour, okay"

"Hey, you're on. Talk to you then."

It was a few minutes past nine when Carolyn and Irv had almost finished her monologue when there was a knock on her door. Mac answered it. He turned to Carolyn. "It's the manager, Carolyn."

"Have him come in. We're almost finished." She said as another crushing roar of a jet engine shook the windows. She looked at Irv and said, "That's as good of an ending that we'll ever get. Wrap it up." She turned and smiled at the manager who looked too young to be a manager of a big hotel. "What can I do for you, sir…how about selling you some soundproofing?"

His smile seemed forced. "You must have heard how they've declared martial law for the county?" Carolyn nodded. He continued. "Well, they have taken over the whole hotel…every room and you have to be out by noon. I tried for the rest of the day for you but they said no. They need the space as soon as possible."

Carolyon frowned. "But I reserved these two rooms for five days…"

The manager's head nodded in recognition of the arrangement. "I told them that…and that you were a news company…but it didn't make any difference to them. I hate to say this, but they told me if you were not out by noon that they would, at the least, throw you out or, at the worst, arrest you for "non-compliance…and that's all I can say…except I'm very, very sorry…my hands are really tied in this."

"Who did you talk to?"

"His name is Major Borgis…he says he's the adjutant for a General Mallory, who I assume is in charge of this martial law thing."

"Well, can you do me a favor…is he in the hotel? If he is, can you ask this Major Borgis to come and see me?"

The manager dutifully nodded with a strained look. "I can do that." He said with a bob of his head as he left.

By eleven, Carolyn and her crew were all packed and ready to go. Fifteen minutes later, a knock on the door revealed Major Borgis, a man of small stature, no more than five foot eight inches even with his elevator heels that Carolyn spied on his army boots so highly polished they looked like patent leather. His camo uniform was crisp and evenly bloused at the top of his boots. His smile was forced and brittle exposing perfect, white teeth. Behind him, two young soldiers, armed with rifles and in camo uniforms. One was Black and the other was White and the tallest of the three. The white young man was quite handsome with full, sharp features, blonde as could be seen with his eyebrows, and with incredible blue eyes like Carolyn's. Both young men looked rigidly straight ahead, and avoided looking at Carolyn except for a cursory glance after they came in.

"The manager said you wanted to see me?" Borgis spoke in a crisp voice, his hands behind his back in the 'at rest' posture with no offer to shake. Carolyn started to speak but then the door opened, and Irv and Mac came in, towels around their necks and wearing boxer print swimming trunks. Carol smiled and introduced them.

"This is Major Borgis, I asked him to come up so I could speak to him about our situation…but how was your swim? …Your last swim in this valley heat?"

Both Irv and Mac smiled. "Great. You should have come with us." Irv said, glancing at Borgis and his two younger companions. For a moment, Irv's eyes held on Borgis and then on the White boy who was now looking intently at both Irv and Mac. Irv nodded at him and then threw a quick knowing eyebrow glance at Mac before coming back to Carolyn. "We're gonna get dressed now. We should be ready on time."

Carolyn smiled. "Good but I'm in hopes we can get a bit more time if the good Major will allow us to."

Borgis's expression didn't change but now he was staring at Mac and Irv and Carolyn noted the only change in his expression was that his nostrils flared as if he was trying to pick of the scent of her companions. "...And what do you two do?" He asked.

Irv shrugged. "I'm her camera man."

"And you?" Borgis asked.

"I'm the pilot."

Borgis nodded. "I guess you've seen a lot out of the windows to impress you. Where did you get your training?"

"Marine Corps...eight years."

"Ever think about re-enlisting?"

"No."

"Why not?"

Mac looked at Carolyn and shot her his captivating smile. "I've got a better boss here. But hey, we have to get dressed and be out of here by noon. So, it was nice to meet you." Mac glanced at Carolyn and then to the white boy whose eyes were now fixed on both Mac and Irv. He looked back to Carolyn and then raised his eyebrows at her in a telling glance with a slight, telling nod before turning to leave the room.

Borgis watched the men leave and then turned back to Carolyn who could see an intentness that made her uncomfortable "I wish there was something I could do to extend your stay but I can't do anything." He told her. "You see, I'm under orders by General Mallory to have this hotel cleared by noon. And your rooms here are the ones the General will be using."

Carolyn managed a brittle smile and then offered her hand on purpose to see if Borgis would take it. He didn't. He only nodded behind his own tight smile and said, "You'll be out by noon then?"

Carolyn couldn't resist the impulse to make the man worry a bit. "Unless I decide to take a swim too." She said quietly behind a feint smile and then added. "You know...this 'visitor thing' might just be broken down and need some time to get it fixed. Have you offered to help them if that's the case?

At the door, Boris did not answer at first but then, hesitating for a moment, he turned and, in a dead pan tone, stated, "I'm sorry, I'm afraid any communications with the visitors are restricted to those on a need to know basis." With that and a thin smile, he left the room with the young Black man managing his own quick almost apologetic smile before he closed the door.

At the Modesto Airport, Mac reviewed the surrounding landscape with Carolyn and Mat to see which direction would be best outside of the twenty-five-mile restricted zone. After calls to Sue in her office in San Francisco, it was decided to go East to the farm and grazing lands outside of Oakdale which they calculated would have the least air traffic in the area. But before taking off, Irv suggested they do a 'plant' with either 'Lucy or Ethel", their two high powered drones that could easily transmit images in the area. Carolyn looked dubious. "I think they'll just shoot them down, Irv."

"Not if we put them in place where they can see but not be seen."

"Where can that happen?" She asked, suddenly liking the idea.

"On top of the hotel…it'll be even better than in the rooms."

Do you think you can get one of them up there without it being spotted?'

"Not a problem." The two men chorused, grinning and nodding their heads. Mac added, "And once they're in place it will be just like us being there."

Irv went further, "But I think we should do it from here at the airport…we'll save power that way too if we get too far out, we'll risk draining her power."

Carolyn nodded. "Let's do it...and if we lose one, we can always send in the reserves."

Packed and loaded with suitcases and equipment, If there was anything to deflate her confidence, it was the unexpected appearance of two men, all in black suits, shoes and hats who seemed to be waiting for them by the door that led to the overpass crossing the street to the covered garage. Carolyn, Irv and Mac gave each other "the glance" as they started across the overpass. "I don't think they think we're really leaving." She muttered under her breath, her face wincing from the day's already insufferable heat as she stepped outside. Looking back, She was right as the two men started to cross behind them.

"Well, I hope they can fly." Mac mused as he slid into the back seat with Carolyn while Irv took the wheel of their rented SUV and switched everything automatic to manual to be more flexible when they hit the heavy traffic,

Carolyn shrugged, looked back at the two men and added with a nonchalant grin, "They're not real. The government insists they aren't. So don't worry...let's make them worry."

In the jammed street, traffic was filled with fearful and desperate people most of whom had switched their electric vehicles automatic features off and resorting to manual controls. Even with that, it took them almost a half an hour to reach the small airport, itself crowded with people wanting flights seemingly to anywhere just to get away from the fears etched into their faces. A family at the auto leasing counter, quickly took their electric SUV after an argument from anther family who said they had been waiting even longer. Loaded with their equipment, and with no baggage helpers to be seen, Carolyn 'borrowed' a luggage cart to walk in the insufferable heat to the hangar where the copter waited. Sweating with their load of cameras, power cords, the two drones, battery cases and transmitters, they packed the copter and then scanned the area to see if they could spot the two men in black. Seeing no one, they jumped into the copter but left 'Lucy" on the tarmac for Irv to trigger to lift once they were safely in the air. At about five hundred feet and after one last scan for the men in black, Irv triggered Lucy to lift off and then watched as their faithful companion lifted effortlessly from the tarmac. Focused on Lucy's screen, he and Carolyn watched the small craft fly swiftly over the traffic and buildings below. In eight minutes, it was hovering over the roof of their hotel and then landing uneventfully with its focus on the same view they had of the 'space-place'".

"Oh…that's beautiful! Caroyn exclaimed watching the monitor's screen just as one of the fully armed copters flew by not a hundred yards from Lucy. It seemed to not notice Lucy at all. Confident and fully fueled and with Lucy safely ensconced on the hotel roof and recording and sending only to their receiver so no one could intercept the transmission, Mac lifted the copter up to cruising height and headed east toward the low foothills of Oakdale. Below, the steady stream of electric cars and truck stood almost at a standstill due to the glut of traffic. After not even a half an hour of cruising, they spotted a farm with a house and barn set back from a narrow road on a long driveway and Mac set the copter down behind the barn. In a few minutes, Carolyn had worked out a rental deal with the owners who helped cover the copter with a large blue hay tarp and let them sleep in the barn, even spreading out some hay for them to sleep on.Still sweating from the effort and the temperature still over a hundred and five degrees, they worked together, grimacing and grunting, to unpack and then hide the copter from any attempts to follow it. Sweating heavily, Mac laid back on the hay in the shade of the barn and suddenly started laughing. "You know, I think the owners here would have paid us to stay here once they realized you were the person walking on top of the big beast. You should have been tougher, Carolyn."

Both Carolyn and Irv chuckled at the idea. "Hey," Carolyn retorted, I'll let you do the negotiating next time!" Still smiling, she added, "But you're probably right from the way his two daughters were looking at you two."

Mr. B

"Yeah, Mac..." Irv added, "...but you could probably have worked a deal with that Major, too, from the way he was looking at you. I mean you could have had a nice bed with no hay!"

Mac made a funny face as Irv laughed. "He had his eyes on you too, compadre. You see he wasn't wearing a wedding ring?"

"Oh...you noticed that too?" Carolyn interjected.

"And his security guard, the big guy," Irv added. "...for a security guard he sure had a look of insecurity on his face when he was looking at you, Mac! I think his only thought at that time was 'Competition'!"

Carolyn laughed. "Oh you two! What a world we live in, guys... you are so perceptive...I don't know what I'd do without you! But right now? I'm exhausted...but you know? What I'm worried about are my sons. I've tried three times to call and all I get is the usual... 'We're not available now, please try your call later'....I want them home...I mean what if this thing out there is not something we can just joke about but is something very, very serious for a mother to think about."

Irv shook his head. "Well, if it is something serious you also might consider they're a lot safer where they are than here, you know?"

Carolyn shook her head, agreeing. "No...I guess it's the mother in me. They're just boys...I mean seventeen and thirteen...what do they know? Huh? I mean I really don't want them with 'him'.... you know? He's not their dad. He's never adopted them, and it really bothers me when I hear them call him 'Dad". Years ago, when I suggested adoption, he dismissed adopting as just a piece of paper. He said, 'It's love that counts' but he left out the word 'money'. I've told the boys how much it bothers me to hear them call him dad but they just shrug it off as not being important. My oldest son even admitted he wants them to call him 'dad' ...almost like he does it on purpose...I feel like he's taking credit for something he's had nothing to do with. No, you don't know my first husband..." Carolyn let out a deep sigh. "He was a real father and so, so good for them...he loved them beyond life itself and sometimes I really beat myself up for marrying again.... especially to Merl.. You know I don't talk about this very much but you don't know what he did after they got there...he called and said, "Oh, I forgot to tell you...I'm going to need some extra cash so I can show the boys a good time.' Do you know how much this good time cost me? Fifteen thousand...he said all of his money was tied up in investments?"

Mac whistled. "You sent it?"

Carolyn nodded. "Sure, I mean what choice did I have? Either I sent it or he'd blame me for their having a boring summer. You don't know him, guys...he's a grade 'A' schmuck...God, I as so dumb! If this whole thing goes upside down and we have to fight for our lives you can bet the first thing he'll do is call and ask for more money so he can 'protect" them. No, I want my boys home! Marta warned me about him but I didn't listen." Carolyn bit her lip and shook her head in regret and then reached over and gave Irv a pat on his shoulder. "I'm going to try and get some sleep after I check in with Sue. You guys should do the same but eat something out of our 'lunch pail'." The check-in between her and Sue lasted, with retakes, until almost four that afternoon, and, after eating a roast beef sandwich and drinking a can of V8, she closed her eyes and laid back on the soft bed of hay. In fifteen minutes, both Irv and Mac could hear her deep and even breathing and knew Carolyn was soundly sleeping.

Seeing this, Mac and Irv laid down on the soft hay, rolled to face one another, with Mac saying quietly, almost in a whisper, "If I ever see this guy I'm not gonna say a word. I'm just gonna gut punch him right then and there!"

Irv let out a quiet snicker and then he gave Mac a soft kiss and a comforting pat and then confided, "She's the only woman I would die for." Mac nodded and then both joined Carolyn in their own weary sleep until darkness set in for the nigh and Carolyn seemed to come awake in her dreams around two in the morning, with crying, moaning, growling to the point the boys sat up and stared at her in the light of a small flashlight to see if she was okay.

A few minutes before three she seemed to settle down except for a few bouts of leg thrashing which also quieted down at a few minutes past four. The two men tried to lay down and get some sleep, but the early morning sun slipped through the boards of the barn at a few minutes past five almost the same time as Ethel's alarm went off signaling a change in what Lucy was detecting. Irv jumped up to look at the monitor. His eyes widened in excited alarm. The space-place was starting to gradually move, and chaos was erupting all around it. Below on the streets, helicopters on the perimeter streets were firing up and police and sheriff vehicles came alive with lights and sirens. Irv held up a finger to his lips and motioned for Mac to come and look. Mac sucked in his breath and looked down at where Carolyn was still sleeping. But as he turned to Irv questioningly, Carolyn seemed to come alive. She sat up looking confused as if she didn't know if she was still dreaming or something real was happening. Irv was the first to speak.

"Carolyn, take it easy...relax...it's just started to move!"

Carolyn jumped to her feet, staggered a bit, and then joined her boys hovering over Ethel's monitor where they could see the huge machine begin to pull at the thick wire restraints flung over its top and dangling down its sides to anchors being yanked out of the cement sidewalks.

"My God!" She whispered as she watched the pandemonium erupting on the streets below. "Set Lucy free! I want to see everything!"

Irv's fingers deftly hit the keys and Lucy responded almost immediately, lifting off over the side of the hotel and moving up towards the top of the space-place where it caught panic-stricken army staff desperately trying to board a dozen or so helicopters stretched along it's length. There seemed to be a jerking lurch that sent men and women screaming and sprawling and then scrambling to their feet in a panicked attempt to reach the closest helicopters whose blades were already whirling, with some already a few feet above the space ship's surface. To the credit of the pilots, no one was left on the surface as the great ship picked up speed, with machines and monitors left behind to form a falling avalanche on those below.

"Sue! Sue! Are you getting this!?" Carolyn cried out, almost yelling.

"Yes! We're getting it! It's unbelievable!"

"Make yourself a copy and hide it. The friggin' government is gonna want to seize it if they know about it!"

"In the process and being done as we speak! Cut this off because you may be monitored. Be safe!"

Carolyn's face went blank as she realized now what the to men in black might represent. She turned to Irv with a frightened look on her face. "Do you think those men in Black could have bugged our copter?"

Irv's blue eyes widened with alarm. He looked at Mac and instantly they jumped out of the copter and began an exterior search while Carolyn examined every inch inside. She was the one who found it, a little box painted helicopter green attached to another green box with no label on the back wall behind a seat. In small print, the label warned: "Do not remove under penalty of law." She pulled on it and felt the magnets give way with little effort.

"They did!" She yelled, tossing it out onto the grass where Irv picked it up and examined if carefully before showing it to Mac. Mac came over to where Carolyn was sitting.

"Where'd you find it?"

Caroyn pointed to the larger green box. "Right here!"

Mac shook his head. "This one isn't it. This is a fake...it's the big green box we have to pull out....and quick...because 'I'm sure they can hear everything we say. Get back!" He told Carolyn and then lifted his foot up and gave the box a hard kick. Once. Twice, and the two small screws holding it from the inside quickly gave way. Mac picked it up and examined it and then announced, "It has a transponder, they even made it look old...but it'll tell them exactly where we are. We've gottta leave now as they're either on their way or hopefully still caught in traffic...so let's get going!" Mac took both of the boxes and dashed across the field to where the landlords old red Chevy pickup truck was parked. He opened the passenger door and tossed them under the front seat. In a moment he was back grinning and panting. "They won't find them until we're long gone but we're just going to have to lag a bit to find Lucy. Ethel is the only one we have now." Mac looked at Irv as he started the rotors. "Can we pick Lucy up?"

Irv grinned. "Did you ever see Lucy fail? Grapes or candy, she could handle it!"

It was almost seven in the morning when the giant spacecraft picked up a little speed, reaching fifty miles an hour going north on McHenry which the ground pursuit had no trouble with. But when it turned east over highway 120 toward the town of Oakdale, it kept the same altitude, but its speed increased to almost a hundred miles an hour, a point where ground pursuit had to be called off. But the horde of pursuing helicopters had no difficulty and floated along side the giant beast like those little fish swimming beside a huge, almost black, giant shark. Even at the height it was flying, the force of the headwinds damaged a lot of trees and roofs until it cleared the town of Oakdale and moved out into open country. And down below, with no warnings coming through on any medium, the people in the fleeing traffic on the ground were caught completely off guard with cars and trucks being blown off the highway along with people on bikes, scooters, and even on foot being blown unexpectedly to the ground.

Keeping his distance to three miles away and parallel on the south side of the huge ship, no one in the CNN copter could see where it was heading and Mac shook his head in confusion. "There's nothing out here, Carolyn. We need to stop and pick up Lucy or her batteries are going to give out."

Carolyn shrugged. "What then?

"Well, we pick up Lucy and catch up but if big bertha there decides to head for the stars when it hits a really big open space, we're just going to have to wave goodbye."

"And if it keeps going this way?"

Mac shrugged. "Well, we catch up and follow it until we get low on fuel and have to turn back."

"Where would that put us?"

"If it keeps going this way? Best bet is we can make it up past Sonora, maybe a town called Twain Hart…but that's about it. We can turn back and fuel up in a little spot called Columbia."

Carolyn took a deep breath. "Let's stop and pick up Lucy and then just take it from there. How does that sound?

Irv nodded. "Sounds good. I can hear Lucy panting."

Mac landed in an open field and they waited, getting out to stretch their legs but once again groaning in the hot summer heat until Lucy caught up and landed about twenty yards from their position. Mac went to pick her up and then jerked his hands back. "She's hot! Really hot."

Irv took in a deep breath. "Well, what do you expect. She's mad as hell."

Carolyn looked at Mac, then Irv, and shook her head, trying not to laugh. "Can we put her in with us? Safely?"

Mac followed Highway 120 on its southern flank and stayed three miles from the spaceplace as it moved steadily up the road at about ninety miles an hour. With their cameras focused on the action, Carolyn and Irv were able to see and record real time what was happening as the giant craft flew above the traffic which was virtually trapped on the narrow road. Some vehicles slammed on their brakes when they finally saw it coming up behind them while others tried to weave in and out to make some kind of headway. But in truth, Irv and Carolyn could only watch helplessly as the carnage only seemed to multiply especially as the road snaked into the foothills.

"Where in the devil is it going!?" Carolyn finally exclaimed. "There's nothing up here!

Mac shook his head. "No...we've got Jamestown coming up and then a rather steep climb up to Sonora. It's really going to get hairy when we reach that point."

"But there's nothing up here.' Carolyn repeated. "They've got the Sonora prison off go the left which we just passed and coming up is Jamestown with its casino, then comes Sonora with another casino up the road a bit more...and then you have Tuolumne off to the right a bit. Do you think it's going up to the lake at Pinecrest...or maybe even Mammoth Lake at the crest? They say it still has the potential to become a volcano and I've seen stories on TV about how the ancient cities with old volcanoes near them have been visited by UFO's speculating they gather renewal energy from them. I mean what else could it be?" She looked at Irv and shrugged her shoulders. "I mean if this is it, we might as well wrap it up and turn around now."

Mac slowed the copter and moved over closer to the road and edged his way into the ring of armed copters forming a circle around the huge craft as the hills rose up and blocked their view. "Let's take a closer look." Max said in response to Carolyn's suggestion as two of the larger and more ominous looking copters yielded to him. He cleared his throat. "We're coming up on Jamestown now." He said to no one in particular, his voice tight with the strain of tension. Then in a stomach dropping move, he quickly descended out of the ring of copters to where he was now flying in the shadow directly underneath the monstrous ship.

"Finally, some shade." Carolyn managed to joke but and Irv said nothing, but their mouths were open in surprise as none of the other copters followed him. Quite suddenly, aa if the huge ship had slammed on its brakes, the formation stopped as the road from

Jamestown rose up sharply in a steep grade leading to Sonora. Below them, in the shadow of the giant craft. the traffic struggled even more desperately to flee up the grade, some even bumping, even smashing, into other cars in attempts to push them out of the way while others dutifully turned on their headlights in the unexpected darkness. Then, with the traffic at a standstill with paralyzing fear, people began jumping out of their cars abandoning their cars and started running back down the highway toward Jamestown while others chose to stand and fight with a number of small arms banging away amid the louder sounds of some heavy rifles. Mac hovered in place about midway under the craft and then let out a little gasp of surprise as further up toward the front of ship, a red line appeared for about two hundred yards, centered, and side to side on the bottom of the ship and then extended further down the length of the ship until it formed a large square which suddenly opened like a giant cassette slot closest to them. As a trained pilot, Mac estimated it to be at least three hundred feet square. Slowly it opened more until the three of them could see the edge of a silvery disc emerge. Mac quickly backed down and descended to where he was no more than fifty feet above the roadway, and tp where he could see people climbing on their cars and frantically motioning for him to come down lower so they could climb on the copter's skids. Then, holding their breath, they watched as the full disc emerged, and it too lowered down closer to the roadway until it almost touched the steep rocky sides of the cut on each side of the road. It hovered there, perhaps two hundred feet above the stalled and frantic traffic where some brave souls held out their camera phones and shot pictures instead of bullets or cowered in or beside their cars. With Mac intent on controlling the copter, Carolyn and Irv stared open mouthed as they watched the silvery disk open a portal in the center and then shoot a beam of greenish yellow light down on an old pickup truck where the young driver stood on the running board taking pictures. Then, in a fraction of a moment, the driver seemed to fall totally limp, but he didn't fall.

Instead, he seemed suspended there as a young Black man who was his passenger scrambled out and across the bed of boxed vegetables in the back of the truck's bed and grabbed him around the waist. The light suddenly pulsed and the young man holding the driver seemed to be pushed down and himself fall unconscious while driver's limp body rose up and into the opening amid screams that came to stop firing for fear of hitting him. In a moment, the body of the young man disappeared into the silvery disc which then rose up six hundred or so feet and inserted itself back into the slot in the bottom of the mother ship. Then came the silence of awe and amazement where nothing or almost nothing moved on the ground or in the air for almost fifteen minutes except the most fearful who either kept firing or tried to flee on foot or by car. Irv kept his cameras rolling, recording and transmitting back to the studio while Mac and Carolyn took pictures with their own phones. Then, with the disc gone and with young man somewhere inside the humongous craft, the monstrous ship suddenly accelerated straight up and in a matter of seconds it was gone and was no longer in sight.

"My God!" Was all Carolyn managed to say until she looked down and started to cry. Then, lifting her head, she looked at her two companions and saw tears streaming down their cheeks too. It was a helpless moment for all of them. With one last glance down below at the mass of people and cars with crumpled metal and plastic, Mac bit his lip and, in a quiet voice one could barely hear over the copter's engines, he said, "I'm going to get some fuel."

Leaving the carnage below behind, they flew in stunned silence, feeling the truth of their helplessness. Carolyn let her eyes drift over the passing land below. In all her years of covering the West Coast for CNN, Carolyn had never been to Columbia State Park although it was close to the airport. Years ago, she had come out to Sonora to cover a mass shooting at the annual county fair and now seeing the huge stones and boulders rising out of the earth reminded her of the head stones for the twenty-three people who had perished in that onslaught...with the same types of guns that were fired at the giant ship that had just taken one of their own. She made a note of how the gouged terrain had recovered with new trees and shrubbery from the historic gold rush days that left gigantic boulders exposed from the hydraulic mining. The estimate of least twenty feet of soil and forests that had once covered the land were now long gone with any gold that had been there. . Now, it was only a memory to be seen in old, old pictures, Carolyn looked at the passing ground and she saw it, at least for a moment, as nothing more than shriveled flesh that now revealed the granite bones of the earth below. But seeing the beauty of the rocks, It reminded her somehow of how the Japanese manicured their land with artfully placed stones and vegetation. Nature has a way of turning man's greed into eventual beauty. When Mac landed, Carolyn stepped out of the copter and called Sue to let her know where they were and her plans to rent a car, if she could find one, and return to Sonora to try and find out the identity and background of the young man who had been abducted and the identity of the young Black man who had tried to save him. Then, she told Sue, "We should be coming home by either nighttime or at latest tomorrow morning." Sue was elated and shared the studio's happiness at everything sent to them. Carolyn managed to put a smile on the screen. "Well, that's our job. The boys have been just wonderful."

The sheriff's office, at least the old one, sat on Washington St., the main thorough fare through Sonora's old business district. It occupied the front and first floor of the old county courthouse, complete with six old jail cells now used for record storage and a courtroom on the second floor that looked like it could be used in a movie about the 1800's. Left vacant by a new one in the newer government center up the hill, the front office had been taken over by the sheriff's office as a second, nostalgic location because of its strategic location for the town's business and tourist population, a move that infuriated the Chairman of the County Board of Supervisors Carlton McMillan. as a waste of money when John Sanson was elected sheriff seven years ago over Elliot Mitchell, McMillan's son-in-law. To assuage his ego upon his son-in-law losing the election, McMillan has ramrodded a brassy sign on the side of the old courthouse designating it as a cultural heritage building and that identified him as the "President of the County Board of Supervisors" rather than "Chairman of the Board of Supervisors". John Sanson's name was left off of the sign even though he was the one who suggested it. It was all a part of the local nitty-gritty which Sue was to learn from a stay that was to last much longer than the following morning.

Corinne Sanchez was the receptionist in the Washington Street office, Married to Manuel Sanchez, a Sonora police lieutenant with two teenagers, she was friendly and very efficient and known for a smile that could calm and angry cobra which was helpful when she had to help in processing irate prisoners being processed downtown before transfer to the main county jail. Nothing seemed to phase her except when she recognized Carolyn Rush walk in the door. At first, there was no smile, just open-mouthed astonishment. Not realizing why she even did it, she stood up and just stared in amazement.

"I wonder if you can help us." Carolyn started calmly, quite used to the overwhelming reaction some people had when she met them. Smiling, he voice was calm. "We just witnessed the abduction of a young man by that huge thing between here and Jamestown. I'm sure you've heard of it by now?

Corrine managed to nod and then her smile quickly followed. "Yes...who hasn't? What do you want to know?"

"Do you have his identity by any chance?

"Yes...the sheriff is down there with his father right now. But the main road is still blocked with all the damaged cars. One other way is to take the old way over the bridge over the highway and then circle around to come up behind on the main highway...but I'm sure it'll be blocked too. But the only other way is to go back through town until you come to a cut off called Skunk Hollow Road that will take you down to the main highway in Jamestown. It only goes to the left back down to Jamestown. But before you get to that, you'll see a road called Rabbits Run to your right. It's the only way it goes. Take it and it will take you down not quite a mile to Kelly Walker's place... it's a car restoration business...you can't miss it.

Carolyn nodded her satisfaction. "Good, good! That's a big help. Hopefully we can get some background information if possible. But we don't want to intrude if it's a bad time. It's certainly got to be a strain on his father."

"I can call...and ask?" Corrine said, cocking her head to one side, looking for a response.

"Please do." Carolyn nodded. She waited nervously, drumming her fingers on the old, scarred counter and waited until Corrine hung up.

Corrine smiled her famous smile. "The sheriff said fine. He talked to Kelly who said okay, anything to get his son back."

"Well, we'll do our best." Carolyn assured her. "You've been a big help. Do you mind if you see yourself on TV when we air this?" For the first time, Corrine blushed before her famous smile exploded across her face. Carolyn took that as a "Yes" answer and motioned for Irv to get a good shot.

Driving back through town, the rental car's "pathfinder" told them when to turn on Skunk Hollow Road. Irv waited for passing traffic and then turned left, remarking, "I don't know how they survive in this heat!" He turned to Mac in the front seat. "Is that as high as the AC goes?"

Mac nodded, "Feels just like winter in the city to me." He grinned. "Did you ever hear what Mark Twain said about San Francisco? He said the coldest winter he ever spent was a 'summer in San Francisco'." Mac shook his head and laughed. "I 'd like to have known that guy. I can't wait to get back there."

Carolyn spoke up. "Those good old days are gone Mac. My phone says it's 91 in the city as we speak."

"What about here?" Irv asked as he slowed for the sign that said Rabbits Run and noting the rental car's temperature gauge was obviously not working although the unit was.

"l04" Carolyn answered. "And climbing."

Both Irv and Mac made disparaging sounds. Mac grunted. "I hope this guy has air conditioning!"

Irv slowed down when he saw the big cement block building looming up as they rounded a bend whose view was blocked by a grove of dusty oak trees. The parking area in front of the building and the house was filled with cars but Irv managed to find a space in front of an over hanging row of awnings sheltering plastic bins of vegetables. On the wall, quickly painted signs declared, "FREE!" while a fine mist of water fogged the long display.

To the right, up a gradual rise, steps led up to a large and obviously spacious house in Marksman style, painted white with forest green trim. It looked like something that could have been built in the l940's, well over a hundred years ago. A wide porch with six tapered pillars ran the full length of the front and was bordered with a vivid display of orange and yellow marigolds with some being a pale lemon color that also bordered the stone path leading up to the porch. The front of the house pitched up into an A frame with vents at the top to let the heat escape. On the roof pitches, a solid covering of solar panels on both sides, fully catching both the morning and the afternoon sunlight. Power lines led up into the garden area where another, smaller building stood, painted to match the house.

Irv nodded as he motioned for Carolyn to go in front of him. "This place is very well designed." Then he added quietly. "It says, money, money, money.."

"And hopefully well air conditioned.!" Mac agreed as they stepped into the shade pf or the porch where Caroly knocked on the door. A young, slender Black youth opened the door and flashed a somewhat sad smile and then nodded. "Sheriff Sanson said to expect you. Come in, come in." He said and added with a bigger smile. "Don't let all the cool air out."

As Carolyn stepped in she could see the room was crowded with well-wishers but it was still delightfully cool , almost cold, and she nodded to both Irv and Mac with a smile to show her pleasure as a very tall, trim man is a sheriff's uniform made his way over to them, extending his hand to Carolyn. The room fell oddly quiet as he said, "Hello. I'm sheriff John Sanson. Come, I want you to meet Kelly… Kelly Walker…Angel's father. His hand deftly touched her shoulder, guiding her through the now smiling faces the length of the room to where an obviously grieving man was sitting in an overstuffed chair, one of two on either side of a giant stone fireplace with a mantel of a variety of sport trophies. The grieving man looked up, his cheeks wet with tears that would not stop.

Sheriff Sanson spoke quietly. "Kelly? This is Carolyn Rush, from CNN. She called and asked if she and her crew could come over. Apparently, they were in the helicopter I saw when the disc took Angel away. They took pictures…the ones you just saw on TV. She's from CNN and they took very good pictures of what happened to Angel. I don't know if you want to see them again or wait a bit longer when you look at the ones we took looking down the road at the same time. What do you think?"

Kelly shook his head no. "I'll wait, Boss. I don't think I…" Kelly began to breathe really hard, sucking in each breath to where another man stepped in and shook his head no.

"It's too much." The man said. Not now…"

Kelly nodded. "I don't want to see no pictures, I want to see Angel."

Sanson agreed. He turned to Carolyn. "This is Pastor Dave. Do you think there could be a better time?"

Carolyn quickly agreed. "Of course…but I wouldn't have him watching TV today or tonight because my station is going to go full out on this. I can respect his condition but there's going to be massive exposure of this event...it just can't be helped. His son is a focal point for the whole world at the moment."

Pastor Dave nodded and spoke up. "Do you think you could wait until possibly tomorrow? He asked.

Carolyn was quick to agree. "Of course. We can stay as long as he wants."

A voice called out from someone by the front window. "Hey...there's more visitors coming.

Sanson turned and the expression on his face tensed up. He shook his head. He looked at Carolyn and shook his head again. "Hey, the lady in the long pink dress...that's Angel's mom. I can fill you in later on her but do me a favor...no matter what...don't take any pictures of the man in the red sports coat. They're not together."

For a moment, Carolyn looked confused at Sanson's request but then looked at Irv and nodded to see if he had heard Sanson's request and understood. He hit the off button as the young Black man opened the door to let Carolton McMillan in followed by two military officers in fatigues backed up by two armed enlisted men also in fatigues. Then, behind them, when Angela Torres stepped inside, the room fell absolutely silent as she made her way over to Kelly Walker where, after a kiss on his forehead, a comforting hug, she whispered a soft, "How are you doing, Pops?"

Kelly took her hand and held it in his. "Not good, Princess...not good." He motioned for the man in the other overstuffed chair to move so Angela could sit down. She smiled graciously and sat down with the grace of a queenly movie star. Then, she looked up at Carolyn, and smiled faintly with a slight nod of recognition.

Carolyn was struck by the woman's absolute grace and beauty, and she could see where Angel had inherited his striking good looks in the picture on the mantle except her hair was blond over delicate features set off by high cheek bones large green eyes over a delicate patrician nose, and full lips. People stared. It was impossible not to. Dressed, after just coming off of work as a night hostess at the casino, in a long pink sequined dress, she was, save for Carolyn, a diamond surrounded by river rock. Carolyn sucked in her breath and gave Irv another slight confirming shake of her head to film what was happening at the moment. Irv signaled he understood and then his eyes widened also as he saw Major Borgis focus on Carolyn like a hawk sighting a fragile rabbit. In a moment, Borgis had his own camera out and started taking shots of Angela and then Carolyn standing by Sheriff Sanson and Kelly Walker. Then, he took a picture of Mac who noticed and assumed the scowl of a mad dog look.

Ever the politician shaking hands and grinning, Carolton McMillan moved across the room, taking his time, still shaking hands and exchanging pleasantries to finally taking a prominent position by Kelly by standing in front of Sheriff Sanson who, at six foot seven, still stood a head taller than McMillan. McMillan barely recognized Sanson with a quick plastic smile and then held out his hand to Kelly and waited until it was obvious that Kelly was refusing to take it, McMillan, undeterred, patted Kelly's shoulder and addressed the crowded room with a voice accustomed to being wanted to be heard. "My friends, I'm so glad Mr. Walker has all of you here to be of comfort in what is a most unimaginable and trying time. The greatest of imaginations could not conceive of a greater tragedy for Mr. Walker, Miss Angela Torres, Angel's mother, or this nation than to have one its own snatched up in a cold, calculating kidnapping of a young man in front of hundreds of terrified witnesses as well as cameras from a national network. Hearing of this, I had no hesitation in contacting the good Colonel here and his assistant, Major Borgis, as to who and what was involved with a major emphasis on what we as citizens of Tuolumne County and this great country can do to bring this to as much of successful conclusion as possible. Hopefully, as in past situations somewhat similar to this, the body of Angel Torres can be recovered and we can work on a resolution to avoid situations such as this in the future.

Kelly Walker suddenly jerked to his feet and faced off with Carolton McMillan. "My son ain't dead you..." Kelly stopped at Pastor Dave's hand touched his shoulder. Kelly glanced over his shoulder at Pastor Dave, then to Angela, and sucked in a deep breath and stared with tearful eyes into McMillan's impassive face ....he ain't dead you... friggin' idiot!"

Seemingly unaffected by Kelly's admonishment, McMillan nodded, consolingly, "I understand, Sir, I was just passing on the information that Major Borgis gave to me...he said no one, not a single living thing, could absorb the rate of acceleration that craft took off in without turning into...." McMillan deftly turned to Major Borgis to fill in the sordid details. "Go ahead, Major, please."

Borgis shifted uncomfortably and cleared his throat. "As I was describing to the President of the Board of Supervisors...everything we know and have experimented with has shown us that at the speeds observed and calculated for that craft...they would turn any organic material into a state much like "mashed potatoes', and..."

Kelly let out a horrified screaming groan and collapsed back into his chair, clutching his head and blocking his ears. "Get that piece of shit out of my house! Now! I mean now or I'll kill him!"

Sheriff Sanson looked at the Colonel and waited for a moment until he could see that either the Colonel did not know what to do or simply wasn't going to do it. "Major Borgis, I think it's best for you to step outside..." Sanson said in a quiet voice and then waited and looked at the man who ignored Sanson and was looking at the Colonel for a decision. "Now! Major. Leave!" Sanson said in a commanding tone. But when Borgis still remained standing there, Sanson added between gritted teeth, "...or I will put you out!"

Not wanting to seem left out or witness an event he would have no control over, the Colonel nodded at Borgis. "You need to step out, Major."

Borgis eyes widened in surprise at the Colonel's directive, but he obediently did an abrupt about face and stalked out of the room with Kelly yelling after him, "...and get off my property!!"

While he couldn't control the events leading up to Borgis' leaving, it was obvious the Colonel was not about to let his purpose or command slip away. He looked at Sanson with hardened eyes. "I will take command of my soldiers, Sheriff" He said in a curt voice.

Sanson did not back down. "Then I suggest you do it in a timelier manner." Sanson replied in a cool, even tone. Their eyes locked in an obvious duel and at that moment, the Colonel realized there was a standoff he couldn't avoid. He looked at the two armed soldiers still standing at 'parade rest'. "I want you to collect all the cameras and recording devices of everyone in this room...including personal phones." He said with an even voice, adding, "including the Sheriff here."

All eyes suddenly turned to Sheriff John Sanson who seemed to show a bit of a smile before he shook his head and replied, "That's not going to happen."

The Colonel's head tilted back as if he didn't hear correctly. "No? This is a military controlled district, Sheriff. I have complete authority."

Sanson nodded. "Yes, you do...but only with the proper paper work that details all of the information in the seizures...and you don't have that. But if you leave copies of it at my office, I'll do my best to comply."

"And I want the truck the boy was in." The Colonel added.

Calmly, Samson shook his head no. "Again, that's not going to happen either. It's evidence in an abduction and my people have to go through it first...then, when we're finished, you're free to have it and copies of all the paperwork we've written up on it."

"Where is it now?"

"I suspect it's either on the way to the yard or in the yard. But like I said, we can stay in touch on it. The truck is Mr. Walker's property and I suspect he'll probably have some say in what he wants done with it."

The Colonel shifted his gaze over to the young Black man still standing quietly by the door, attentive to everything that was being said. The Colonel nodded at him. "You were with Angel?"

Randy Medine nodded.

"What's your name?"

"Medina, Randy Medina."

"And you were with Angel?

Randy scowled, unimpressed by the Colonel or his uniform. "What did I just say!? He shot back.

"Don't get smart with me, boy, or I'll have them take you in for full questioning!"

Randy scowled. "Hey! Don't be calling me 'boy' either unless you don't want me to cooperate! That doesn't work up here. In fact, screw it! Write me a list of what you want me to tell you and then mail it to me here...cuz right now I'm through talking to any of you guys."

The Colonel looked over to Sheriff Sanson like he needed some help but Sanson just shrugged again. "You're not doing very well, Colonel...the score right now is zero for you guys...and what's with the men in black suits? What are they doing out there with the Major?"

At that, Carolyn went to the window and looked out on the street where Major Borgis was talking to the two men. "They followed us from Modesto and either one of them or Borgis put a tracker in our copter!"

Sanson frowned. "You do that to news people?"

The Colonel shrugged. "I can't comment on that."

It was Sanson's turn to shrug. "Well, let tell you what then...when we get everything settled here, I'll send you a copy of everything we come up with. Just leave me your name...because for some reason

I don't see you wearing a tag.... your address...street and town or e-mail or both...and I promise I'll send you everything we come up with...and that's the best I can do...or am willing to do. So what do you say to that?"

The expression on the Colonel's face remained impassive. Finally, he shrugged. "I'll make note of your lack of cooperation...so I'll think about it and then, in the future, let you know through your 'president' here on the board of supervisors. "I think we'll be dealing with him from this point on." McMillan smiled at the recognition and with that, the Colonel turned to leave without a thank you or any form of sympathy for Kelly Walker's son, Angel, Kelly Walker or Angel's mother, Angela Torres. When he reached the door, Carlton McMillan hesitated to follow him out, but he did have the presence of mind to stop and once again express his sympathy to Kelly Walker and Angela who said nothing and stared the man down with Walker's subtle shake of his head.

Carolyn rolled her eyes when McMillan shut the door behind him. "My God!" She exclaimed, "What's this country coming to!?" She turned to Irv. "Did you get any of that on tape?"

Irv grinned. "All of it except the guy in red." Then, with a doubtful look, he slyly asked, "Do you think they'll shoot me?"

Carolyn bit her lip and then burst out laughing and then closed her eyes and pumped her fist in the air and then went over and hugged him saying, "Thank you! Thank you! Thank you! God!" She told him but then added, "But don't worry, Irv. I'll have a wonderful eulogy for you!"

It was almost five when the last of the people left Kelly' place after sharing parting moments of anger and sympathy over what had transpired earlier. Had he been there, Carolton McMillan would not have been a happy man.

When the room finally cleared, only Sheriff Hanson, Kelly, Carolyn and her crew, Angela and Randy Medina were left. Angela smiled and went over to Caroly and held out her hand. The two women gently embraced one another and Carolyn confided, " I have two sons of my own but I can only imagine what you're feeling right now if they've been watching any of this.

Angels drew in a deep breath and looked out the window to the street below where the last of the cars were pulling away. She turned back to Carolyn. "Thank you… but you can't imagine my feelings now…Kelly can I guess." Her expression became wistful. She looked at Carolyn and reached out to touch her arm. " But you know… I can still remember and feel the pain of giving birth to Angel…but it's nothing like the pain I feel now." She turned back to Kelly who was staring at her from his chair. "Kelly? She said, hesitating for a moment, "…do you have anything I can take home with me of Angel's?"

Kelly sat quite still for a moment, and then he nodded and looked at Randy questioningly. "What do you think, Mijo?"

Randy hesitated for a moment and then smiled. " I can get you one of Angel's Bible for you? He has three."

For the first time, Kelly managed a slight smile and nodded his approval.

Randy's head jerked agreement and he disappeared down the hallway. Angela then turned to Sheriff Hanson. "I'd ask you to come visit for a bit…just for old time's sake but I still have Boo and Booboo with me and you know they are not really fans of the police"

John Hanson showed his understanding with a slight grimace. "Well, the feeling is mutual, Angela… but it's no problem but I have to say it's good to see you looking so good again."

Angela smiled winsomely. "And I guess I could say the same for you. It's been a while. Too long. I'm still at the casino…nights."

Carolyn held out her hand to Angela. "It's so nice to have met you. I was wondering…since I won't be leaving until tomorrow, would it be possible or me to come by sometime tomorrow morning and do a quick interview with you after work?"

Angela looked questioningly at Hanson. Does she know about my room mates?"

Hanson shook his head no. "But I can fill her in tonight. Maybe you two would better like a phone call or meet someplace else?"

Carolyn was quick to agree. "Hey, I'll give you a call and we can set something up. How's that?

"That would be fine". Angela replied, taking the Bible Randy held out to her. She looked at it and then lifted it up to give it a kiss before pressing it against her chest. "I think I'll be needing this much more often now."

"We all do," Randy offered. There was a genuine sadness in his eyes.

"Amen." Pasto Dave added. "Call me any time."

Originally, Carolyn and her crew had not planned on spending the night in Sonora but faced with still having to interview Randy and his relationship with Angel Torres and what happened during the abduction, and now an additional interview with Angel's mother, Angela, they decided to stay. And flying home in darkness was not something Mac wanted to do which caused another problem and that problem was that, because of the massive influx of refugees, there wasn't a single room or camping sight to be had in the entire area, including the casinos. Kelly was the first to speak up, offering his place but Carolyn was not comfortable with Kelly's offer to let her use Angel's room with Irv and Mac sharing Randy's room. With that impasse, Sheriff John Sanson spoke up that his place had two extra bedrooms, but they would have to put up with his dog, 'Husky", who was a genuine Alaskan Husky in the middle of severe shedding in the summer's heat.

"But I make a mean breakfast." Sanson added to counter the idea of a hairy Husky. "...and I do wake up early. And if anyone wants to go for an early morning run around five...you're welcome to join me."

With that, Mac held up his hand, declaring, "Hey, count me in!"

Sanson's house was a small somewhat Victorian structure with a steep peak over the rounded front door. Carolyn took it all in, noting the same necklace of Marigold flowers around the perimeter as the ones around Kelly Walker's house. Sanson seemed to be aware of the comparison and commented, as he unlocked the door, "Angel and Randy take care of my yards."

Carolyn nodded. "They do a good job."

Inside it was refreshingly cool due to the solar panels which, like at Kelly Walkers, were placed on both sides of the peaked roof to catch both morning and afternoon sun. Everyone seemed to take in a deep breath and give a sign of relief from the heat. The solar roof panels were now a common and most necessary fixture in the area with the obvious global warming which almost no one doubted any more. Then, from the kitchen came a single somewhat startling clapping sound and in walked Husky into the living room. Going first to Sanson, tail wagging happily, he enjoyed the brisk rubbing on his shedding fur as he looked around at the visitors. Taking his cue from Sanson, he assumed everyone was safe and welcome and so began his visiting rounds, enjoying the additional petting until he ended visit his with Irv when Sanson uttered one word. "Bed." Husky immediately returned to sit by Sanson's chair where Sanson picked up his phone and called out for dinner. "I hope you guys like chimichangas." He announced. "A friend down across the street from my office has a restaurant called, Jimmy's Chimmis.' His are absolutely the best in the west. People drive up from the valley just to eat them. And if you happen not to like them, put them in the fridge and I'll have them tomorrow." Sanson smiled. And then added with a another smile, "....and, if you don't, I'll fix you a toasted cheese and ham sandwich." The rest of the evening was spent watching the news on television. "Kind of like watching family movies, isn't it Carolyn?" Irv joked, as her monologue started. When the main program ended with President Pollard rescinding the National Emergency Proclamation and the military restrictions as well as his trip to California to see the great spaceship, there was only a passing word about Angel Medina being abducted as if he was nothing more than a footnote in an unexplainable national mystery. And it was then that Hanson began sharing Angela Torres with Carolyn when she asked, "What can you tell me about Angel's mother. She doesn't look old enough to have a twenty-two-year-old son."

Sanson shook his head and smiled. "Well, I guess you can say she wasn't. But that was Angel's fathers' fault, Diego Torres's, not hers. From what they both shared or confided with me over time, when Diego saw Angela, he was totally smitten with her beauty when he first spotted her as a sophomore walking home from school. Even though he was twenty-two and she was just fifteen, he decided he was going to have her...and he did. Diego was a shot caller in a gang down in Compton...being in the news business, you know what a shot caller is...he didn't deny himself anything or anyone, including Angela. Well, when he learned she was pregnant with their boy, Angel, I guess Diego started to have a change of heart about his lifestyle and how he wanted to raise his son. He worked for an auto rehab house working mostly on low riders and that was how he learned on the internet about Kelly Walker needing a new man to help him out in his auto rehab business here in Jamestown. He had an old, even at that time, fifty-nine Buick Electra hardtop convertible fully strapped out and looking better than the day it came off the factory floor almost a hundred years earlier. So, one day without telling anyone except Angela they left for here in Jamestown. No goodbyes. Nothing. He just left the past behind. Angel was just two at the time. Diego didn't even tell his parents because they were deep, deep into the family gang life...drugs, guns, you name it. Well, when they got here and Kelly saw Diego's car, he hired him on the spot and gave them a trailer in his trailer park just down the road there on Rabbits Run. Something seemed to catch on fire in Diego and besides working for Kelly, he got a part-time job working for the casino's security on the night shift. That's where he met what Angela calls the BooBoo boys, Travis Sorenson and his own boy, William who my whole department knows as Chilly Willy because the boy is stone cold when it comes to feeling good or bad about anything... an absolute sociopath. Even when Willy was put into juvenile hall at fourteen, the county psychiatrist shared that in her opinion, Willy has no conscience...no emotional attachments to anything, people, animals, even his father, nothing. He was an absolute zero. Well, going back a bit, Travis sees Diego's beautiful old Buick and they strike up a friendship. Travis, who likes to be known as 'Dog", has this sad tale of woe about how he and his boy are living in an old, abandoned trailer with no heat or air. Again, Diego's old brotherhood habits come back to haunt him and he decided he wanted to help out an old struggling "brother' and invited him and his boy to stay with him until they can get back on their feet. Little Chilly Willy is about ten years old at this time and Angel would be about eight. With Diego's help, Travis gets a part-time position in the Casino security and Travis just falls more and more in love with Diego's old Buick which draws people wherever they go. He offers to buy it and make payments and Diego laughs and tells him the car is worth over a hundred grand and that even he couldn't buy it. Well, a year later, Diego is shot dead on duty at the Casino. We couldn't figure out why. No motive, nothing. It goes cold except Travis tells everyone that Diego told him that if anything ever happens to him, Diego wants Travis to have his car, and even shows Angela a type written note supposedly signed by Diego. When we ran the note through our lab, it showed Diego's signature was pulled from one of his checks and was a bit off color from when Travis photo copied it. And can you believe him? No. Everyone laughs at him. But he keeps insisting. And here's the kicker…when Angela pulls out the owner's registration on the car and looks at the bottom, she sees where Diego has sold the car to his son, Angel, for the sum of one dollar. And Angel's only ten years old. It's his inheritance and Diego even wrote that on the DMV form. Instead of accepting this when he learned this, Travis goes wild. We had to lock him up because he was either going to hurt himself or someone else. Unbelievable…just unbelievable. And Angela still lets them stay there because she feels sorry for them. When I asked her why, she looked at me and shrugged and asked me where they could go. Travis lost his job because he didn't show up for work because of what he said was his grief and mourning over Diego's death. I'm sure Angela can fill you in on more of the details, but I'd avoid being anywhere close to them as Travis is a con artist of the first order and I really think he'll try and put a move on you. Trust me on that and you can take it to the bank…just not McMillan's."

In the morning, Sanson and Mac went on an early morning run with Husky while Caroly and Irv cleaned the kitchen from the evening dinner. At six, when Sanson returned with Mac, they set their itinerary with Sanson calling Elliot Mitchell, his assistant, to take over command for the day while Hanson accompanied Carolyn back to Kelly's house to interview Randy Medina for the coming night's special on CNN. And being so close to where Angela Torres lived at a trailer park down Rabbits Run, Caroly told Hason she wanted to interview her there as well after interviewing Randy, providing Angela was willing. "I'll take my chances with Dog and Willy, the Boo Boo boys.. Irv and Mac will have my back." She assured Sanson.

"Well, I'm going to be right up the road if you should need me... and maybe when you get back I can show you guys my own re-hab down in the garage. Been working on it for years with Kelly."

Suzzane smiled. "That sounds great! Then maybe some lunch before we leave?

Sanson smiled. "You got it...but it's got to be Chimis. I am totally hooked on those things!"

Carolyn finished her interview with Randy by ten and left down the road for Angela's house, arriving just a few minutes before ten thirty due to Irv taking the time to load all of his sound and camera equipment. Angela's trailer home was absolutely finished to "the nines"...perfection in an eighteenth century opulence from gold scrolled furniture to elaborate print silk drapes festooned with fringe. And when Angela answered the door, she reflected that same sense of perfection, still dressed in her long casino silk dress like a Kimono from the casino. And again, when her door opened, the same cool air greeted her that seemed to be prevalent everywhere Carolyn went. But she had not seen any solar panels on the roofs and Carolyn was prepared for the worst until Angela explained, they were set up on racks in the back yard facing east and west to catch a full day of sunlight. Angela further explained the old roof style wouldn't accommodate the weight of the panels or the electrical intricacies required for the installation. Carolyn shrugged, grateful for the comfort. "Cool is cool...no matter what." She smiled and then was taken aback a bit when she saw the two men sitting on the couch, their eyes riveted on Carolyn who managed a smile even while remembering Sanson's warning. But when Irv and Mac followed her in, their attention softened substantially to one that almost appeared to be resentment.

Angela nodded in their direction. "They just had to meet you." She said, with a feint smile. They know you from watching TV. The gentleman on the left is Travis Sorenson and then other young man is his son, Willy. They have to go out job hunting, but they wanted to stay to meet you in person."

Travis Sorenson stood up and walked over to Carolyn and offered his hand, holding Carolyn's hand until she made the effort to pull away. Travis turned to Willy still sitting on the couch. "My son here was a good friend of Angel. We both was quite upset with what happened and of course we want to do everything we can to help out Angela here because she's done so much for me and my boy here... he's a special needs boy you know and that ain't easy."

"Of course. How well I know." Carlyn agreed. " And that's good of both of you. But I don't want to hold you up from your job hunting because it's going to be even hotter again today...almost a hundred and ten. So, it was nice meeting you...and good luck."

Travis Sorenson stood there for a moment as if he had more to say but realizing he had been really cut off from saying whatever had been on his mind as Carolyn turned to Irv and started giving set-up directions as to where she wanted to film and record which included the couch where Willy was still sitting, staring at Mac and Irv.

"You guys married?" Willy suddenly asked, not getting up.

Mac stared at the younger man, feeling exactly the same as Irv was as he arranged the receivers around the room to focus on the beautiful satin couch. Mac shook his head, "Nope, not yet."

Willy persisted. "Where you guys live?

Irv answered without even looking at Willy. "We live in the city."

Willy grunted. "San Franscico?" He leaned forward to show his interest.

Mac nodded. "Yeah..."

Willy let eyes shift from Mac to Irv to Mac to Irv. "Do you think I could come and visit you guys sometime?"

With a quick glance at Irve, Mac was the quickest to shut Willy down. "I don't think so, Willy, I mean we're hardly ever there...I mean look at us right now. We're here in Jamestown and tomorrow? Who knows where this lady is going to drag us off to. And it's very expensive living there. Did you go to college?"

Willy shook his head. "Nah...it's too expensive."

"Well," Mac went on. "If you want to live in the city, you gotta have at least a degree in something or you're going to be on the streets. And the streets in the city are a lot harder than they are here…I can tell you that right now. I think I heard that five guys didn't make it just last night. It was just pop, pop, pop, you know?"

Willy laughed. "Hey, I pop with the best of them!"

Mac shrugged. "Well, if you're that cool, you might look Irv up some time to see what's what…right Irv?"

Irv spun around and glared at Mac who was grinning devilishly at him. Irv shook his head almost violently. "You remember I'm dying of Solpheriaisphelangiaitis don't you? Or did you forget!?"

Willy's eyes widened in alarm and the expression on his face twisted into a mixture of alarm and confusion. "What's that?" He asked quickly, looking at his father, now open mouthed, who gave him a helpless shrug.

Irv shook his head and held up his hands like he didn't want to talk about it. Then he turned to Willy. "It's new and they're not exactly sure what causes it yet but it's like the old HIV but much worse and faster. When I get excited or very tired, I start coughing and it's like it doesn't stop…. bloody phlegm…and gobs of boogery snot…and it goers everywhere. My last roommate caught it from me in less than two months, but he couldn't get on the program or afford the medicine so…it was just tough….I…" Irv shook his head and looked away, biting his lip, and then at Mac to finish it while Carolyn, finally catching on, stood there with her hands on her hips, staring at the two of them in mock disbelief.

Carolyn held up her hands for her two men to stop. "You know, Irv, the only reason you are my assistant is because no one else would work with you. Your meds are working but the program you're on pays for everything…and that's the only reason they say you're still alive." She turned to Willy. "I think you'd have a wonderful time staying with Irv but it's an experimental program, Willy…and you know what that means."

Willy quickly nodded. "Yeah...Yeah...it was just a thought, man. I, uh, I uh... I'm gonna find a job here and see what happens." Willy got up from the couch and pulled on his father's shirt to leave when Irv started to cough. And when Irv stepped forward to wish him luck, Willy quickly stepped back behind his father to avoid taking Irv's hand when Irv held it out. Willy followed his father out with a cautionary look over his shoulder when Irv began coughing again. Only when they heard the back door slam and the old electric car whir to start did any of them dare to laugh. Angela looked at them in complete confusion.

"How can you laugh at a situation as serious as this?" She asked in an admonishing tone. Her gullible innocence only made the three of them laugh all the harder.

But while Angela soon found the humor in the ruse, she turned the interview into a mind bender when she confided, "I know who killed Diego and why."

Carolyn, Irv and Mac stopped everything in stunned silence until Carolyn asked, "What do you mean? You really know or just suspect?"

Angela shook her head. "No...I know.:"

Caroln leaned forward, her voice almost a whisper. "Who?"

"Willy...."

"But Sanson even said he had an alibi...air tight...you."

"I did...but I didn't know I was lying at the time. I thought I was telling the truth until a week after it happened Willy came up to me and warned me not to change my story. He didn't say he actually did it at the time but I realized what he was saying...that he did it. And worse, he seemed proud of it...like he'd done me a favor."

"My God....!" Carolyn exclaimed. "Angela, let us get finished setting up. I want to get this on tape. Willy was just a kid when it happened wasn't he?"

Angela nodded. "Yeah...and I think you can see that he still is 'just a kid'. But he did everything his dad wanted...everything...and some of it was so gross...and still is...that I don't want to talk about it. His dad trained him to be what he is."

"Oh my God! That's terrible, Angela....you've got to tell somebody! Irv! Are you ready?"

Irv motioned to his equipment and gestured it was all set and running.

Angela shook her head, seeming not to care she was being recorded. "Travis knows that I know. I told him so because right after Diego was killed, he warned me not to change my 'story' or he'd have Angel killed too. I just knew right then and there it was them. I looked at him and told him that if anything happened to Angel that I'd kill both him and Willy myself."

Carolyn shook her head in disbelief. "But they're both still here living with you, Angela. How can..."

Angela shrugged and gave a little smile before she interrupted Carolyn. "How can I kill them if they leave...and they have no where to go. I pay for everything...everything. They can't go anywhere, and I make good, good money." She gestured at the elaborate furnishings that seemed so out of place in a trailer. "Here they have everything...but it's a prison for them. They're afraid to leave and afraid to stay. And me? Well, with Angel gone now...and they had nothing to do with that... they don't know what to do...or what I might do. Travis even assured me that he had nothing to do with Angel being taken...you see, he's so afraid...and so dumb that I would think that what happened he could be responsible for it. No somewhere I read a guy who said keep your friends close and your enemies even closer...and that's what I'm doing now. And Willy? He's as much a victim as Diego was. He can't survive anywhere else. He's like a puppy in traffic. Sooner or later, he's gonna get hit and killed."

"Angela...? How did they do it?"

Angela sank down into the beautiful silk covered sofa and closed her eyes as if she was looking back into the past. Then, staring intently at Carolyn, she began, "Travis..'Dog'? He's dumb as dog shit but he's cunning. Whatever woman gave birth to Willy is lucky to be so far out of their lives. And that night? All of us rode together to the casino in

Diego's old Buick. Every time, it was like a parade when we got there. People just crowded around. They just couldn't believe the car was so old, so beautifully perfect, and ran on gas and was so big and just so incredibly beautiful. They just don' t make them like that anymore.... It was Diego's pride and joy. He lived for it. But it would also be a part of Travis's scheme to kill him. You see, the day before that night, Wilily complained of being sick so Travis tucked him in bed and he still complained he was sick. The next day. Angel went to school but Willy stayed home. But that night, before we all left for work, he stayed in bed there for a bit before crawling out his window and climbing into the huge trunk of the Buick. I didn't know. When we got to the casino, Diego parked in the preferred parking lot because the casino owners liked him and liked to use the car in the local parades. Well, Travis had given Willy a map that showed the places and times of Diego's security route. He hid in a corridor for deliveries only used during the day. So when Diego came by that corridor for his route, Willy stepped out from behind him and shot in the back of the head. The police called it an execution style murder and suggested it was revenge from his old days in Compton...and they went with that...with Willy drinking beer and sleeping in the trunk, waiting for his dad and me to take him home in the morning. It was all so clever that Willy couldn't keep his pride in check and bragging just a week later how now his dad was going to own the Buick. I didn't see how that was going to happen until I asked, and Travis showed me the note that Diego supposedly signed giving Travis the Buick. But when the sheriff's department examined the note and said it was fake...that their machines showed the signature was on a piece of paper of a different type and color and glued onto the note itself...and then run through another copier, showed It was fake. And then the old DMV change of ownership paper I pulled out of the glove box gave the car to Angel when it showed where Diego had written that the car was to be his inheritance. Well, Travis went ballistic when he got the final word. claiming the court was prejudiced against him because of his record. He got so mad and bad with drinking and drugs that he had to be locked up for three days just to calm down...but he still claimed that "someone" was out to get him...and that's where it all ended. Kelly took the car into storage and that's where it's been till this day."

"What did Angel say about Willy not being at home?"

"Nothing. They didn't get along at all. Travis and Willy slept in one bedroom and Angel slept in his. He didn't even know that Willy slipped out and went with us." The next morning after Travis and I got home, Willy snuck back into his old room. No one knew. No one.:

"Wow! No one suspected a thing...and you've kept all this in to yourself since your husband was murdered?"

"Yeah, at least until I finally figured it out when Travis and Willy kept warning me not to change my testimony on Willy. I mean, why would I...but they were both so worried..." And listen, I expect you guys to keep it to yourselves too...and let me handle it my way . "Travis is really worried about what I might do now that Angel is gone. And I want him to feel that."

Carolyn let out a huge, anxious sigh. "Well, I can see why. But I don't know what to say, Angela, except that even your life could be in danger now. Everything you've told me is now a part of a record. A crime's been committed. I can't change that."

"But you don't have to broadcast it do you?"

"No...you're right about that. Not right now. But eventually....especially if something should happen to you...I mean I think you should think about both your husband and your son, Angel. I think you all deserve the truth."

Angela looked at Irv and Mac with both nodding agreement with Carolyn. She gave a little shrug. "I'll think about it...but until then you'll all keep quiet?"

It was Mac who spoke first. "Yeah, but I wont lie if anyone asks me." He said, speaking for both Irv and Carolyn whose heads bobbed in agreement.

Back at Kelly's, it was a somber trio that came into the house and sank soulfully into the couch and one of the stuffed chairs. Their expressions did not escape -Sanson, Kelly or Randy.

"Looks like it didn't go very well." He offered and eyed Carolyn.

She shook her head. "No, it didn't," was all she offered back.

"Wanna share?" Sanson looked first at Carolyn and then to Irv and Mac. All shook their heads no. With a shrug, Kelly left the room to go into the kitchen.

Samson let out a sigh, Well, if and when you do, just let me know. But would you like to see my surprise down in the garage?"

Mac nodded. "Yeah...and I want to see that old Buick too if we could."

"No problem. Randy? Can you get the keys from Kelly. He has a lot of wonderful surprises tucked in down there...including mine. So common...I think it will cheer you up."

-The heat of the day was now more than just a promise. They all shifted uncomfortably while Sanson worked the lock and punched in a security code. Then with Randy's help, he slid the squeaking door to the right and stepped back to let them in to the cool interior. The first things visible were Kelly's work area but beyond that, the cavernous area showed at least a dozen cars parked side by side, shrouded under tarps.

"Which one is Diego's Buick?" Irv asked.

Sanson gestured to the right in the back. "The last one on the right." Can you show him Randy?"

Can we take the covers off?" Mac asked as Randy led them to the rear of the building past the rows of treasured vehicles.

"Sure..." Randy replied. "But just be sure to put them back the way they are."

"What are all the rest of these?" Carolyn asked as they made their way back to the end the building.

Mr. B

"All gas models…no electric…most are from the fifties and early sixties, but he has an old 1948 Cadillac convertible…and I think there's a 1939 Lincoln Phaeton too…at least I think that's the year." Randy told them.

At the last covered vehicle, Mac and Irv stared at one another. "You want to help me"" Mac asked, picking up the left corner of the tarp. Irv nodded and they slowly pulled it off front to rear, gasping at both the size and beauty of the machine as it was slowly revealed.

"Oh whoa!" Carolyn murmured. "It's huge!" She declared as Mac and Irv pressed their faces to the windows. "Can you imagine cars like these cruising down the highway? They look like pieces of art! And look how the red interior is accented with the white outside paint. Beautiful, just beautiful!

"They are." Came a voice behind them at the entrance. They turned and saw Kelly standing there and, for the first time, smiling. "You want to see my favorite? Take off the tarp on the one next to Diego's Buick…. it's a 55 Pontiac Star Chief."

Irv and Randy carefully removed the tarp to reveal a two toned, two door hardtop model with two tone paint of bronze on the bottom and cream on top. Inside, the upholstery and door panels matched the exterior colors. "No grey paint at all!" he declared and then turned to Mac who gave a shake of his head in awe.

"Can you imagine what it must have been like in those days? I've seen it on TV but this is the reality. No wonder Travis wanted it so bad." Mac said quietly in a church like whisper… can I sit in it?

Kelly nodded, grinning with pride as he came down the center aisle, casually pulling off tarp after tarp to reveal the sparkling jewels of his collection, reciting the names and years of each model to the utterings of amazement from Carolyn and her crew. Kelly turned back to the front and pointed to a tarp he hadn't pulled as yet. He motioned for Sanson to come back and do it. Sanson grinned with pride.

Sanson turned to Carolyn. "How would you like to take a ride in this today?" He asked her and pulled the tarp off to reveal a gleaming two-seat sports car, painted red with a black leather interior. The wire spoke wheels shined like diamonds and a white line on the tires set them off. "It's a 1960 Austin Healy....English...six cylinder...and almost finished except for the wind wings that go on the sides of the front windshield. They've been on order for months now....and probably will cost as much as the car did when new. The top is folded into the back." He turned to Mac. "Would you two like to learn how to drive it?"

Mac threw up his hands in surprise. His mood from Angela's was gone. "Oh God! Are you serious?"

Hanson laughed. "Have I ever lied to you before?"

Irv shook his head in disbelief. "Just give me the keys and I'll take it from there!"

Sanson laughed again. "Hey guys, Carolyn comes first. But remember, it's a stick...not an automatic like today's cars. And it's gas, not electric."

Irv shot Sanson a look of humor. 'Hey, living with Mac, I know what gas is! He smirked and then clasped his hands together prayerfully and looked up at the roof. "Just give me the stick and I can do it!"

Lunch at Jimi's Chimis up in Sonora came and went with a reluctant Kelly at first but deciding to go if Randy went. It ended with great acclimation from Carolyn and her crew who ordered two more orders to go. "With rice and beans." Mac added. And then with Irv adding, "You see? Now you know where the gas come from!" Mac grabbed Irv on the back of his next until Irv groaned fake agony and pulled away, laughing.

Earlier, It was decided to go from the restaurant to the airport in Columbia so with Sanson and Carolyn leading the way in the Austin Healy, while Irv, Mac, Randy and Kelly followed in the little "Charger", the electric rental. The road twisted through the pine trees jutting up between the giant boulders exposed by the mining for

Mr. B

gold over two centuries ago. At the airport, Mac and Irv transferred their equipment from the car to the copter with Randy volunteering to take the car back to the rental station not a quarter of a mile away.

With the copter loaded, everyone shook hands and hugged with Carolyn lingering to the last before she quickly stepped up in front of Sanson and took his face in her hands and pulled him down to where she could kiss him. It caught Sanson by surprise, but he grinned.

"Hey," he said, still smiling. "If you come back, maybe we can do another one.

Carolyn laughed. "For sure! I've been waiting to do that since I first saw you!"

"Well, why did you wait for so long?" Sanson shot back, laughing as the rotors began to spin. They caught with a roar, stirring up the ground dust and making everyone shout and squint.

"When I come back with my boys, it will be first on my list!" She yelled and waved as the copter lifted up.

Sanson, Kelly and Randy watched the copter until it disappeared over the tree line on the distant hill. With one last wave, Sanson settled behind the wheel of the Healy and followed Randy to the car rental office. But then, a few minutes later riding back on the road to Sonora, they heard the sound of a copter and looked up to see a gaggle of arms waving out of each side before it veered off to the west. With Randy tucked uncomfortably behind the two seats, he patted Sanson on the back. "I think she likes you." He grinned.

The warm, comfortable feeling of being liked…loved…did not last long. Back at Kellys, Sanson and Randy helped Kelly pull the tarps back over his beloved car collection with Sanson lingered to rinse the dust off of his car and gently rub away the bug splatters on the windshield , the headlights, and the front grill before wheeling it inside the shop and covering it with a final, loving pat. Kelly and Randy had already gone inside when his phone rang with the news that a young man had been found dead in his room at the Casino. Elliot Mitchell was there handling the investigation. Sanson passed through to him.

"Elliot? Sanson here."

"Hey, Boss…thanks for getting back to me. We've got a messy one here. Nothing left but the body. Everything was taken…absolutely stripped. Maid found him. Had a do not disturb tag on his door but she finally opened it up because he wasn't responding to her knocks. He's been brutalized… physically and …sexually. His underpants were stuffed in his mouth and down his throat but no signs of a struggle or anything. We suspect at some point he was drugged. Front desk gave us his particulars and the coroner is on his way up."

"Have you been able to locate any family yet?"

"No, too early. Front desk says he listed Stockton as his home address and the photo on file of his driver' license copy shows he just turned twenty-three. It looks like robbery and predation…of the worst kind…mutilation…and he was emasculated…his manhood is missing. We're going through the security cameras now and the ones from the second floor where his room was show three men going into his room about eleven last night but only two came out about four hours later. And they knew what they were doing because they were all still shrouded with dark shirts and hoodies. Look like the Bobsy twins from the dark side. Can't see a thing. The car he was driving is gone too so we're checking the outside camera's too."

"You want me up there?"

"Nah..I don't think so. We know the routine. Andy and Bestrum are with me. Hey, we won't let you down."

"I'm not worried about that. Amigo. How about the cameras on the floor or the restaurant,. Lighting is really good there."

"We checked. Nothing there. We see the victim mostly by himself, He cruises the floor, looking around, kind of trying out the machines to see which ones feel lucky but later there is another man who comes up to him…and it looks like one of the guys leaving the room, the shorter one.. He's all in black…with a hoody but it's weird here because the one shot we get of the new man we can't tell diddly because it looks like he's wearing makeup of some kind…with eye glitter, rouge and lip stick. And it's like he knows where the cameras are. He keep his back to them and his head down under his hoodie. They talk for about maybe five minutes and then they leave together and meet up with the other mystery man in the hall with the elevator and go back to his room. The elevator cameras don't show didley either. The two guys never look up. We talked to a lot of the guests on the floor but no one seems to recall either one except a young man who says the victim approached him earlier and asked if he'd like to get together later…so we kind of know what he was looking for."

"Yeah…but a lot more than what he was looking for…what kind of car was he driving? Have you put it out yet?"

"Yeah, It's a newer Chinese Sassoo. Two door, silver…"

"Well, it sounds to me like you've covered all your bases, Amigo. Call me if anything new comes up or if you think I can help in any way."

"How'd your day off go?"

"Great…until now. Talk to you later."

Sanson took a deep breath and headed for the office downtown. Whatever happiness he had felt just hours ago was now gone, only to be buried even further when he pulled up to the office and saw Carlton McMillan's red Cadillac SUV pulled up…in Sanson's space with other spaces available just two spots over. Sanson parked in an empty space and got out of his car and waked over to his space, took a picture, and pulled out his traffic citation book and wrote out a ticked and slipped it under McMillan's windshield. He managed a hard grin when he imagined McMillan leaving and finding the ticket. He doubted he would come back in but rather go straight to Judge Henry and try and get it written off with some type of excuse. But

Sanson would kill any excuse he would come up with by offering Judge Henry pictures of the four available spots.

Inside, adding insult to injury, he found Supervisor McMillan sitting in his office...and worse, sitting in his chair behind his desk. More worse still,, McMillan tried to shut the sliding drawer in front as Sanson waked in. Sanson glowered at the man and then tersely commanded. "Get out!'

McMillan, flushing a bit, got up and then tried to sit in one of the two chairs in front of Sanson's desk but Sanson shook his head. "I didn't say 'move'...I said get out!" He snapped.

McMillan's head jerked back in a gesture of pride and he made no effort to leave. "I'm the President of the Chamber of County Supervisors! I can sit any damn place I want! This is all County property!"

"And if you don't get up and out, 'Mr.President', I'm going to have my men sit your ass back in another part of County property... one of those empty cells and charge you with illegal entry and you can take it up with Judge Henry when you see him later!"

McMillan managed to stand but he made no effort to leave. "I'm not seeing Judge Henry today. I have no reason to."

Sanson smiled. "Really...well we'll just have to wait and see about that. Now get out and don't come back unless you have an appointment. Right now, I'm busy and you really need to leave."

McMillan stood quite still for a moment as if trying to decide what he should do. Fnally, watching Sanson sit down and start going through his center drawer, McMillan turned, saying nothing, and left.

In the hour before Judge Henry's call came in, Sanson spent the time reviewing the situation at the Casino but found nothing that Elliot had not told him about. He punched the button on his desk

Mr. B

screen phone and found the always serious face of Judge Henry staring at him.

"John? Supervisor McMillan is here and more than a little upset that you gave him a ticket. Is it true?"

"Yes Sir. When I pulled into the back of the old courthouse here, he was parked in my spot. I know it sounds petty but it's not the first time it's happened and there were four other empty spots he could have taken…but he chose not to. I sent you pictures. He just likes to strut his stuff. Then when I came into my office, he was sitting in my chair behind my desk and going through the center drawer. I'm not sure if he took any candy or gum or not so I can't charge him with burglary, but I told him to leave, and at first he refuse until I threatened to arrest him for illegal entry. Here again, from my shoulder camera, let me show you how he was parked and the spaces that were available." With several clicks, the pictures popped up on the screen. "I know you can void the ticket but quite frankly I've finally had enough of his omnipotence and would appreciate it if you could find the 'huevos' to stick it to him."

Judge Henry did not smile or laugh very often, and when Judge Henry did, Sanson was surprised to see he had all his teeth. Judge Henry finally stopped laughing but still smiling, announced, "I'll take care of it. It's done."

Later that day, Corine called Sanson to tell him that McMillan had his daughter come down to the County Clerk's office to pay his ticket, under protest of course. Sanson shook his head in disappointment over how little the man could be and still act like he was powerful. Feeling the heaviness of McMillans behavior, Sanson said a prayer for him. A serious prayer, because, like the men in his jail, he felt the burden of the man's moral poverty.

If Sanson had any hopes that the troubles he was required to face would lessen a bit, he was wrong as the next morning Angela called and asked for him to come down to her place. She said she had something to show him and also wanted to talk about what she and Carolyn had discussed the day before. Sanson agreed, wondering what Angela and Carolyn had discussed and that Carolyn had not shared with him. He pulled in front of her trailer and spent a few minutes just looking around, marveling at how well Kelly had the boys maintain the grounds with mowing, trimming, and of course the beds of flowers. Kelly was an extraordinary man and his influence on Angel was more than obvious. To see him so obviously crushed by Angel's abduction was a burdensome pain. He vowed to get down to see his friend more often.

Angela met Samsom at the door a little sheepishly with a shotgun in hand. "This isn't for you, John…but I had a little problem here last night while I was at work. Come in and let me show you." Sanson instinctively ducked under the doorway although he would have cleared the top by several inches. He followed Angela into the small kitchen on the far side of the room and stopped as she pointed to the microwave on the counter. "Would you open it for me? I did it once but I won't do it again until someone sees what I saw."

Sanson gave Angela a studied look for a few moments and then pushed the open button. It popped open but not enough to see in until he opened the door. His face wrinkled in surprise and disgust. "My God!" He murmured and shut the door and turned to Angela who patted her shotgun. Inside was a dead black and whiite kitten, cooked to death, juices still liquid in the turntable.

"Now you know why I carry this" She said quietly, patting the shotgun again. "Eve though they didn't sign it, I know it's from Travis and Willy…they left a note". She pulled the sheet of paper from under the microwave and handed it to Sanson.

"Hay Sweet. Sorry you wuznt here when we stopped by. Jest wanted to show you what hapens to people who cant keep kwiet."

Sanson looked at it again and then folded it up and slipped it into his shirt pocket. He shook his head. "Can't say nobody warned you. I'm gonna keep this and put out a BOLO for the two of them and have them picked up. I'm sure we can find a way to get them to write something we can use to compare both their writing and spelling... and then we can charge them with making dangerous threats as well as cruelty to animals...this is just sick"

Angela agreed. "I know...I just cried and cried when I saw it."

"Why don't you go and sit down while I take some pictures. Do you feel like writing down what you found and saw for me? I'm gonna need it for the record...and seeing you with that shotgun... do you think you should stay here until we can find them?

Angela looked at Sanson and smiled. "I hope they do come back because like I told the CNN lady, I know they killed my Diego. This thing has two shots in it. I mean why else would they say they were going to kill Angel if I changed my story about Wllly being home that night? I had no reason to. I believe them until they threatened me and Angel. Then I wasn't hard to figure out."

"You gonna tell me?"

Angela shrugged. "Don't want to because it makes me live through it again.' She sat down on the couch and stared into space like a looking glass into the past. "... Willy said he'd been sick all day... so when we left for work, I came in and kissed him goodnight and told him to get some rest...and Diego was with me He gave Willy a pat on his head and said if it really got bad, to call because he could bring Travis home. And the irony of it was that Willy listened to all that concern and knew all along he was going to kill Diego...for his dad...because they wanted Diego's car." Angela shook her head in disbelief and took in a deep breath. "It was all planned. John When we closed his door, he was out the window and jumping into the trunk of Diego's Buick. After shooting Diego, he jumped back into the trunk and stayed there all night...drinking beer and listening to his headset. It really worked well for them but the note saying Diego wanted to give Travis his car was his downfall...I thank God for that and you guys seeing it was a forgery. But still you guys still thought it was a grudge killing from his old gang in Compton. Even Angel believed that. He didn't have a clue and I never told him anything I began to feel."

"But it you'd told us when you found out, Angela, we could have done something..."

"Not in time to save him. I didn't knw! But while you guys were doing your 'something', I had a son to protect if I said anything...I wasn't gonna risk losing two them...no way. And besides, it took me some time to figure it out...I really wasn't looking to find blame...just bury my husband and do the best I could. Now? It's different."

"Yeah, I can see that...but now's the time for justice to step in...but we gotta prove it with evidence...not your version. A good defense lawyer will tell the jury that your version is just nothing more than suspicion because Travis wanted Diego's car. Do you really want to stay here, Angela? You know you could stay at Kelly's?"

Angela shook her head. "No...You'll take the kitten?"

"Yeah. You gotta plastic grocery bag?"

When Sanson drove back up to Kelly's to share Angela's story, Kelly slipped into a deep, funky mood and he punched himself on his knee as if to punish himself. "I never liked those guys, never. There was always something sneaky about them no matter what the situation was. They was always trying to play the angle."

Sanson agreed. "Yeah, you're right, Kelly. But at least I get to slap them with cruelty to animals now."

Kelly looked away in disgust. I don't need this now, I really don't."

"None of us do but at least I can take them off the streets for awhile. That's worth some satisfaction…" Sanson stopped as his shoulder phone buzzed with Elliot shown as thecaller. .

"Hey, what's up, Amigo?"

We've just about finished up here on the guy that got emasculated and we were able to contact his family down in Stockton with the help of the front desk. His sister asked if we found the kitten she gave him but we didn't. She said he takes it everywhere with him. I told her…"

"Stop! Stop! Stop! Amigo. What color was it?"

"Black and white…about two months old…but…"

Sanson took a deep breath and interrupted Elliot. "Elliot, Elliot…I have the kitten but unfortunately, it's dead. Dog and Willy cooked it in Angela's microwave last night while she was at work…and left a warning note…but the kitten's head was cut off first so I don' t think it died in there."

Elliot made a gruesome sound. "My God! Are you serious?"

"Totally. So you need to put out a BOLO for both of these guys with a homicide attached to it"

"Hey , Boss….some good new on that. Those guys are here right now, in the casino, supplying some guys from Silicon Valley with women….and I'm sure drugs are involved too.."

"Hey, " Sanson bit on his tongue and then said, "I wanna come up so don't let them leave."

Elliot managed to laugh. "I don't think they'll be leaving any time soon. This crew they're with has money. The guy in charge owns a big AI company and is here treating his top people to all the comforts the devil can provide…the owner's got a huge vacation home on wheels taking up two spots and hasn't responded to Security to move it or to keep the noise down in the suites either. Security asked if we could help so I'll tell them you're coming up. That should make them happy."

"Elliot, Elliot, don't let them move that trail bus. Find a way to immobilize it. If you have to puncture tires, do it! I want Dog and Willy to go down with this! Comprende? Give me thirty…but if they should come out of the room, take them down!"

"Gotcha Boss."

Sanson clicked off and looked at Kelly." Hey, compadre? How would you like to go back on 'shore patrol' with me, huh? I think you caught enough of what I was saying, and I can fill you in on anything you missed."

Kelly timed it to twenty seven minutes when Sanson squealed into the parking lot of the beautiful casino at ten forty three and saw his man Rudy flagging him over to the parking lot for the big motor homes where two more of his men stood by, guns drawn. Thinking ahead, Sanson pulled in behind the huge motorhome on the far side and out of sight of anyone coming from the casino.

When he exited his patrol car, his face was serious to the point of grim. "Still inside?"

Rudy nodded. "Yup..,and still doing wild."

Hanson had Rudy come with him and Kelly and they took the staff entrance into the back rooms for deliveries and eventually access to the main floor. But at a door marked 'private', Hanson was greeted by a portly middle aged man who looked Indian and a younger man, trim, with dark eyes and sweating heavily. The older man's badge identified him as Geroge Mondo. The second and younger man wore a badge identifying him as Thomas Ahern, Security Chief. From them, Hanson was shown the layout of where the rooms were on the fourth floor and what access, if any, they had to the outside other than the main hallway which had three elevators, one in the middle next to an alcove with an ice machine, just two rooms away from

Mr. B

where Dog and Willy would be, and one at each end of the hallway where an exit door stood next to another ice machines and a sign alerting guests to to the stairs for an emergency exit.

Sanson was quick to take charge. He told Elliot to post a man inside each elevator as well as on the landings just below the fourth floor with orders to capture if possible or shoot if necessary. "No man is to leave his position until they get orders from me or Elliot." And then he added, "No men are to go on the gaming floor either and invite shoot off with the guests down there. Elliot and I will be on the fourth floor by the center ice machine when Casino Security will make an effort to get the men to leave their rooms to check out in thirty minutes.... under the pretense that if they don't, you will call the Sheriffs in...understood?" Sanson asked, looking at the head of security, Thomas Ahern, and added. "Remember, these guys are dangerous. They've already killed one man here."

Ahern's wiped his brow and nodded. "Where do you want me?" He asked.

"You'll be the man at the door. You identify yourself...and take someone with you. Show a sign of strength."

Ahern sucked in a frantic breath. "I'm not even armed..." His voice trailed off to a frantic look of lip biting worry.

"I don't want you to be....if you're not armed, no one inside will feel threatened. This is gonna look like a normal request to leave. Understand?"

Ahern nodded with a worried glance at the casino manager. "What time do you want to start this? He asked, giving Hanson a doubtful look.

"Let me get my men in position and then I'll give you a call to head on up...okay? We should be ready in no more than ten minutes...but I'll call. You'll be passing my men or Elliot and me on the way up."

In his call to Ahern, Sanson confirmed his men were in position and ready. But he got no answer from Ahern, On the second attempt,

Fools Of A Privileged Kind

a strange voice came on asking who was calling. Sanson scowled." I'm calling for Ahern. Is he there?"

"No, He left."

"Oh my God!" Samson steamed. "Is the manager there?"

"He's in the bathroom. Can he call you back?"

"Loyd was just here but Ahern sent him up to fourth floor to ask some people to leave."

"Are you serious?" Sanson asked, incredulous.

"Yeah...who's this?"

It took a moment for Sanson to recover. "That's alright...I'll take to Loyd. Thank you."

With no response from Lloyd, Sanson turned to Elliot and shook his head, whispering, "We're playing our wild cards now."

Samson and Elliot heard the elevator open and then shut and peeked out of the cubby hole with the ice machine and vending machines to see a young kid knocking on the first door. The kid waited and then knocked again, stepping back when the door opened suddenly. He handed whoever answered the door a note of some sort and then, stammering at first, managed to say, "You gotta be out of here in thirty minutes or they're gonna call the sheriff."

The man responded with an ugly curse and then slammed the door as hard as the hinges would allow.

Screw it," Sanson growled and stepped out just as the door opened again and a thin, and pale white man with a black beard and mustache, dressed in boxer shorts and carrying an ice bucket, stepped out into the hallway. Seeing Sanson, he screamed in a high pitched girly tone

"It's the police!..., The police!" and tried to slam the door shut but what little strength he had after his scream was useless against Sanson's strength and bulk. Sanson stepped into the room with Elliot right behind him, gun drawn. The four men in the room froze, stopping their frantic efforts to clean up the residual powders on the nightstand that had been drug out to the center of the floor for universal access. In a quick glance, Sanson saw three of them hold their hands up but the fourth seemed more defiant. Sanson's eyes swept the room for anyone else hiding but didn't see who he was really looking for...Travis or Willy Sorenson. Sanson motioned for the more belligerent man to open the connecting door to the other room. When he complied, he stepped back, and Sanson and Elliot found themselves facing two other men, their faces frozen in fear with Travia and Willy holding guns to their heads...and grinning. Behind them, two young women lay nude on the double queen beds, their fear not letting them hide their nakedness

Grinning, Travis swore. "You need to get out or the real party's gonna start, pig!" He tapped the barrel of the pistol hard against the wincing man's head.

Sanson did not waver. "You need to put your guns down and just come out, Travis...the party is over."

Travis shook his head. "If you want to drag more dead bodies out, just keep standing there because we're leaving!"

Sanson shook his head. "You can leave with those two but everyone else stays here...including the women."

Travis hesitated, thinking about the offer. He shook his head. "Give me that one there, the owner." He said, nodding toward the more belligerent man whose eyes suddenly widened in terror.

Sanson didn't hesitate. "Done." He looked at the man who now had lost all resistance and started breathing hard in terror.

"I'm not going with him!" he said, in a now, almost squeaky voice.

"If you don't, he's going to kill the man right there. If you go, the others here, including the ladies, are gonna have a chance to live. I'll do the best I can to protect you, but you have to know that these two are already wanted for another murder right here."

Travis and Willy swore almost in unison. "What are you talking about?! Travis growled first.

Sanson looked at Elliot and then back to Travis. A feint grin pulled his lips. "A little kitten told me."

The expression on Travis' face seemed to go into shock. He glared at his son, Willy. Then, he turned back to Sanson. "Give me him and then I'll leave with these two...but give me at least ten minutes."

Sanson nodded, "Done..." He grabbed the owner by the arm and shoved him at Travis who quickly put the gun to his head and shoved the other man past Sanson and Elliot.

"Ten minutes!" Travis repeated, stepping toward the door of his room to the hall. "Is there anyone out there?" He demanded.

Sanson nodded. "Yeah but I'll call them off."

"Lemme hear you do it!"

Hanson complied and hearing it, Travis added just as the stepped out into the hallway, "But if you're lying, these two are dead! Guaranteed!

When Sanson was sure that Travis and Willy had left the floor, he turned to the two women and four men frozen in place. "Get dressed and then stay here. He tapped his shoulder camera. "I have you on film so don't think you can get away..." With that, he motioned for Elliot to follow him and the two ran down the hall to the stairs where one of their men was still waiting to join them as Sanson ordered. "All units to the parking lot!"

The glaring noon sun hit them full force as they ran across the parking lot toward the huge motorhome sitting there with all the tires on the drivers' far side flattened but unseen at first by Travis, Willy and their two hostages when the owner tried to start the vehicle and put it in gear. A gun shot rang out in frustration when the owner alerted Travis to the flattened tires showing up on the status screen. Sanson turned and saw Rudy writhing on the ground, holding his lower leg. With no hesitation, he drew his own gun and fired back at one of the blackened windows where he could see the glass was broken and then quickly ordering Med-Vac service while two of his men ran to pull Rudy to safety. The vehicle's row of darkened windows made it impossible to see who might be behind them except for the one with a bullet hole. Travis or Willy...it made no difference to Sanson whose men had now taken cover behind other motorhomes. This was now a kill or be killed situation. But suddenly there was a loud booming sound from a high caliber weapon like the one Kelly had brought with him. And after the explosion, Hanson could see the spray of blood on the shattered glass on the passenger side. Then he heard Kelly's yell.

"All clear!" As the door on the passenger side opened and Hanson saw the owner and the other hostage stagger out and collapse gasping on the blazing hot asphalt, not caring about anything except being free. Hanson ran toward the two crying men and helped them to their feet, fearing the massive spray of blood and tissue on the owner was his but further examination showed he wasn't injured, at least physically. Sanson then called the Casino to report an "all clear" situation and need for medical assistance.

Still cautious, Sanson crept around to the far side of the motorhome and found Kelly on the roof of a smaller motorhome, belly down in the sniper's prone position. He waved to Sanson and then started to get to his feet while Sanson examined the broken driver's side window where a small spray of blood hinted at the carnage inside. Going around the front, he could see the blood and tissue spray expanding to where it looked as if someone had spray painted the inside. He stopped at the door as Elliot came up to him. Together, they stepped inside, avoiding stepping on as much blood and tissue as possible. On the far side in the driver's seat, the faceless Travis leaned back as if relaxing while Willy' face was shattered but intact except for the back of his skull which was gone in a spray of bone, blood and brain on what was left of the window behind him. Sanson hesitated, chastising himself for his thoughts and then, with a shake of his head, they began taking the obligatory pictures to add to whatever the coroner would take.

It was almost four in the afternoon when the scene was wrapped up and the coroner took the bodies of Travis and Willy to the morgue. Angela was the first person Sanson called. It was brief by her choice but very thankful. Then, Sanson placed a call to Carolyn whose phone told him she would call back. Elliot and a detachment of men had taken the six men and two young women to the new jail for processing and Sanson went to his office to begin compiling the lengthy reports, starting with the kitten followed by Elliot's call alerting him to the situation at the casino, the kitten, and revelation that both Travis and Willy were there entertaining a group of men from Silicon Valley with women and drugs. It was almost six when he finished. Then it was off to the hospital to check on Rudy where he learned the bullet had gone through muscle tissue in his left leg and exited with no bone contact. He would heal fairly quickly.

At home, he tried calling Carolyn again but got the same results which was not what he wanted. He made a face of disappointment. Still on edge from the day, Sanson got in his car and drove down to Kelly's just to be around someone comfortable. Inside the house, he laid back on the couch and watched TV with Kelly and tried to get his mind wrapped around the events that had taken place. Then, Sanson hunched forward and stared out the front window as daylight edged into night. "You know, Kelly," he began, "I think this is gonna be it for me. I'm tired."

Kelly looked over at his old friend and nodded. "I know the feeling. I came home and decided one simple truth. You wanna know what it is?"

Sanson looked at his old friend and smiled. "Hit me with it."

"Life..." Kelly began, "...is pure shit...with a lot of sugar on it in some places. I guess the happy ones are the ones who haven't licked their way through all the sugar."

Sanson's eyes met Kelly's and they both laughed. Sanson shook his head. "And where are we?"

"Well, today we got through the sugar."

Samson leaned back and laughed and nodded. "I have to admit when I saw your shot took out both Travis and Willy...well I was both happy and sad. What a pair of wasted lives, Amigo. Just wasted.

I wonder what they said when they discovered that their lives ended right their...no heaven...nothing? Who'd they blame if they even were given a chance to try to put it on someone else...maybe me. And the men in the motor home?...Well, I think their sugar turned into the shit you were talking about...sad...just very, very sad...for all of them. Hand how about that Ahern guy, head of security. He ran...but you know, no matter how far he runs, he'll never outrun the memory of what he did. I feel sorry for the guy...love the badge and title but there was nothing behind it. Nothing. He's no Rudy, that's for sure."

Kelly agreed. "You wanna come down and work on your car tomorrow?"

Sanson shrugged. "Maybe but I've been trying to get in touch with Carolyn. I'm thinking about taking some days off and I though maybe she'd like to come up and spend some time here."

Kelly looked at his friend and smiled knowingly. "You really like her, don't you?" Kelly asked and Sanson hesitated before admitting that he did with a jerk of his head. Kelly smiled. "It shows, my friend... but all I've go to say is don't let yourself get hurt. She's from a very high level...a lot higher than we are."

It was dark when Sanson returned home and was greeted by an almost frantic Husky who wouldn't even touch his food but followed Sanson around as if he was on a leash. Finally, Sanson cooked two hamburgers and shared them with his companion while they watched the local news with Carolton McMillan playing center stage and just oozing concern for the safety of the county's citizens and being sure to center stage his son-in-law, Elliot Mitchell as the key player in the successful drama. Just listening to the man, Sanson made a face and turned the TV off just as the phone rang. The caller ID showed it was Carolyn. Smiling happily, he punched the play button.

"Hello there!" He said, with a newfound joy in his voice. "Where you been?" He asked.

"Hollister...another terrible school shooting! You know you'd think earthquakes are enough and that they'd start teaching character in

K-12...but no, algebra...which no one ever uses. God have mercy on us! Hey, I saw you called but I couldn't break away...I'm so sorry!"

"Hey, don't apologize...we had our problems here too. You remember Travis and Willy?'

"Yeah?"

"Well, they're not here anymore."

"What happened"

"The old Marine sniper Kelly took them out...one bullet, two men...very fitting but I can fill you in later if you'd like to come up? We may be on TV too; I don't know because it involves a very important man from Silicon Valley. Name's Sumar Gil...from what I hear he's about the third richest man around in the AI business. But hey, I'm thinking about taking some days off...per policy...and I thought maybe you'd like to come up and spend some time hunting gold?"

"That sounds wonderful but, John, my boys are home now and..."

"Hey...bring them with you. I'll teach them how to pan for gold too."

"Are you sure? That sounds great...but if they don't want to come, they can stay home with Marta. Just tell me when. And by he way, just so you'll know...I filed for divorce...John?"

Sanson couldn't respond for a moment but then he managed to say, "I gotta tell you...that's good news! We'll get together on a good time for both of us."

"Good. Just let me know because there's nothing keeping me here except old habits. Except one thing I gotta say."

"What's that?

"Well, God Bless you, John... and...love you."

Sanson laughed and smiled. "I couldn't have said it better myself! See you soon."

For the first time in what seemed a too long of a time, Sanson slept well with Husky curled up at his feet.

Sanson's buoyant feeling of content did not last long. In his office, a few minutes after ten o'clock the following day, Monday, Corrine buzzed him with the news Carolton McMillan was holding on the line for him. Sanson instinctively made a face as he picked up his phone. "Sanson here." He said in a crisp voice.

"Sheriff Sanson? Supervisor McMillan here. I have some news here that I'm holding you directly responsible for from that incident at the casino yesterday."

"Uh huh? What's that?"

"Mr. Sabor Gil's lawyer called this morning and is threatening us... the County...with a five million dollar lawsuit unless we immediately drop all charges and release him today!"

"...And?" Sanson asked

"What do you mean...'and?'...you were responsible for what happened! I'll expect you to come before the full Board to explain your actions!"

Hanson leaned back in his chair and hesitated for just a moment before he replied. "Yesterday I saw you on TV and you gave Elliot full credit for the capture and jailing of six men and the death of two felons. So, what's it gonna be...Elliot in front of the Board or me not taking the time to show up?"

"Damn it! Don't play games with me, Sanson. You're out of your league if you think you can!"

"Hey, you listen to me, Mr. Supervisor...I'm glad I'm not in your league...believe me when I say that. You want to run scared? Go ahead! But I'm not changing a thing in how we handled it! Nothing! So I suggest you get a grip on yourself and get some guts to do what's right! That is if you can find any part of you that has any real courage! And hey...tell that lawyer guy that we haven't decided whether to keep that motorhome or not because it was loaded with drugs. I don't know who brought them, Travis and Willy or the guys who came up in it...but it makes no difference. It's ours if we want to keep it." With that, Sanson hung up, half expecting McMillan to call back. But after staring at the phone for almost a minute, there was no blinking light to show an incoming call. After a few minutes, Sanson called Elliot to let him know what his father-in-law had said.

Elliot's response was quick and emphatic. "Screw him."

Sanson laughed. "You're gonna make a great sheriff when I retire."

Sabor Gil's lawyer posted bond for him and his employees on Tuesday and left town with heads low but not before requesting when a decision would be made on the motorhome. Two days later, when the forensic team had finished their examinations, Sanson watched the huge motorhome hoisted up by the front end and towed out of the holding yard, a blue tarp covering the broken windshield. The cost of replacing the windshield alone was over five hundred thousand dollars, the blown tires on the driver's side over twenty thousand, too much for the sheriff's budget. Sanson was happy to see it go and was looking forward to Carolyn's promise to come up on Saturday with her two boys...just one day away.

Sanson took Friday off and let Elliot run the shop.

To say Sanson was both nervous and excited Saturday morning, was obvious. He anxiously watched the clock over the door between his living room and kitchen go from nine to ten-thirty with Husky happy to have Sanson comforting rubbing while both of them waited on his couch. Finally, at a few minutes to eleven, he heard car doors slam in his driveway and he got up and went to the front door. Opening it, he felt the blast of the day's heat hit him full in the face as Carolyn and her two boys scurried up the sidewalk and into the house. faces wincing in the heat, where they breathed a sign of relief. Sanson smiled and embraced Carolyn while her two boys stood there, scrutinizing the two of them. Sanson offered the

Mr. B

boys his hand and gestured for them to have seats on the couch after warning them to take a pillow to brush off any dog hair.

"I'm John..." He said, smiling and offering his hand again. "And you are...?" He asked the older one.

"Caleb." The young man replied, not smiling but not seeming to be intimidated at all by Sanson's size.

"Antonio." The youngest offered with a confident grin.

"You wanna hunt for some gold?" Sanson asked and both boys were eager in their response but only with head nods and real smiles. "Well, tomorrow's the day, guys. No guarantees but the water is gonna be wet and cold. That part you'll like. Hungry?"

Carolyn laughed. "Always!"

The next day, a Saturday, Sanson drove down to Kelly's to borrow his thirty-six year old 4x4 gas driven Chevy Avalanche pickup to use for the trip up the highway to Spring Gap, a secluded spot almost to Pine Crest and then down, at frequently alarming times, a very steep and narrow one way road cut into the heavily forested mountain side. For the fun of it, Sanson brought along his recorder to monitor the boys' reactions to the jaw dropping, hour long, three mile drop down the mountain to the river. So they would remember the experience, Carolyn recorded them on her camera too, at least when she herself was not bracing herself in her seat and open mouthed with an honest fear as the truck tackled and bounced over rocks and ruts in the twists and turns on the narrow path. At times, Sanson had to smile at the little squeaks and ooohs of concern as the sturdy truck brushed past branches sticking out in their way.

"This isn't the Nimitz Freeway or the Bay Shore." He remarked as the truck took an ominous dip and then a wicked bounce back up." To the sounds of alarming oohs.

"What do we do if we meet somebody coming up?" Caleb asked, staring wide eyed out the front widow from the back seat. Beside him, his brother, Antonio, pulled back from the open window with a little squeaking sound as he dodged a thick bunch of branches from a bush slapping its way into the truck.

Sanson turning Caleb's question into a lesson. "You have your driver's license yet?" He asked.

"My learners permit."

"Well what do you think has to be done if we do meet someone coming up this road? Do we back up or do they back down?"

Caleb shrugged that he didn't know. He looked at Antonio who did the same.

"Well, think about it…who has the greater control…the guy who has to back down or the guy who has to back up the hill?"

The boys again looked at one another and shrugged.

"Hey, ask your Mom…see if she knows."

Carolyn let out a sharp little laugh. "How did I get into this?"

Sanson chuckled. "It's in your learner's manual, guys. You should know it so you and the other driver don't start shooting at each other. Give up?"

The boys were in unison. "Yeah"

"The driver going up hill has to back up.

Caleb made a face of disbelief. "Why's that!?"

Sanson twisted the steering wheel and then punched the gas. The truck lurched up and to the right over some large boulders filing a rut. Back in control, Sanson asked another question for the boys to examine. "Who has better control of their brakes? The guy backing up the hill or the guy backing down the hill?"

Caleb's expression twisted in thought. "The guy going up the hill."

"Why's that?" Sanson asked.

Caleb's smile said he understood. "Because the guy going down the hill has a harder time stopping if he starts to slide than the man going up the hill."

Sanson allowed himself the time to take his hands off the steering wheel to give a quick clap. "Right on! Mijo."

The rest of the day went just as smoothly except that Carolyn was the only one to find a small nugget of gold buried in the silt and gravel on the downstream side of a big boulder. She promised to split it with them…three ways.

Late that afternoon, Sanson stopped at Jimi's Chimis and they all enjoyed a delicious Mexican dinner. Home again, the four of them played with an old set of dominoes Sanson pulled out of a game bag that he often took to the juvenile hall. Sitting at the kitchen table, they played until almost ten when Carolyn held up the blank piece and announced, "I walked on something like this." It was to be a prophetic moment as at a bit past eleven, Sanson's phone rang just as he was falling asleep.

He turned in bed and strained to hear the whispering voice on the other end of the phone. He asked the caller to speak up and it was then he recognized Kelly's voice.

"Boss! Boss!" Kelly rasped. "He's back!"

Sanson, struggling out of fresh sleep, struggled to understand. "Who's back, Amigo?"

"Angel!" Kelly whispered harshly. "He's back!"

"What do you mean, he's back? How"?

"Hell! I don't know! He's sleeping in his room! Randy heard him come in!"

Sanson sat up, now wide awake. "You saw him?!"

"Yes! What do I do? He's right there in his bed!"

"Hey, let him sleep. I'm coming down!"

"Good! I was hoping you'd say that!"

"Let me get dressed…I'm going to wake up Carolyn and bring her with me…and I'll be bringing your truck back too. Give me at least thirty, okay?"

"You got it but just hurry…I don't know what to do."

Sanson dressed in the same clothes as his trip to Spring Gap and then knocked on Carolyn's bedroom door and opened it. She turned in bed and in the light from the hallway, saw Sanson was fully dressed. "What's the matter?" She asked.

"You didn't hear the phone?"

"No."

'' It was Kelly."

"What's wrong?"

"Nothing, nothing but he said that Angel's back...and sleeping in his bed. He said Randy heard him come in."

"You're kidding me."

Sanson shook his head. "I'm going down. You wanna go with me?"

Carolyn swept the single sheet aside revealing a very scanty nighty and grabbed the pants she wore to Spring Gap on the chair by the bed and then pulled the yellow tank top over her head. She looked at Sanson as if she suddenly froze.. "The boys...I don' want to leave them."

Sanson nodded. "Wake them up...but hurry."

The porch light at Kelly's house was on and the lights in the living room illuminate the front porch and the garland of flowers as Sanson and Carolyn started up the steps followed by Carolyn's two boys, wide eyed with uncertainty at the bits and pieces of talk they heard between their mother and Sanson. Sanson glanced at his watch and saw it was a few minutes before midnight as Randy opened the front door before they could knock.

Sanson shook Randy's hand and then spoke quietly. ' You remember Carolyn and these are her two sons...Caleb and Antonio. Where's Kelly"

Randy gestured down the hall. "He's with Angel...he's just sitting there in a chair. I think he's too afraid that Angel's gonna wake up and leave or something...I don't know."

Sanson turned to Carolyn. "You guys wait here. I'm going to go back with Kelly." At the hallway, he turned. "if you guys want something, Randy can get it for you." He glanced at Caroly and saw her pulling her phone out. "Who are you calling?" He asked.

Carolyn held up a finger, asking for a moment while she dialed. "The office. I'm gonna need Irv and Mac to bring my equipment here."

After a moment of anxious hesitation Sanson nodded agreement and disappeared down the hallway. Carolyn waited for the night operator to come on the line. She turned to her sons and looked at them very seriously. "Do you know who we're talking about?" She asked them. They nodded dutifully. "Well, make sure you handle yourselves well, okay?" Again they nodded and took seats on the couch as Carolyn's hand directed them.

In a few minutes, Sanson returned, shaking his head in amazement. "Its just unbelievable....totally!" He said, looking at Carolyn.

Carolyn agreed but added, "What about Angela? Shouldn't we call her?"

Sanson nodded. "And Pastor Dave."

"Irv and Mac should be here between nine and ten. They wanted to know if they could land in the field beyond the garden."

"Tell them yes. No problem."

Carolyn nodded and dialed her phone while Sanson first called Angela, still at work at the casino, and then Pastor Dave. He offered to have one of his men on patrol pick up Angela but she said she'd drive down as it would be much faster.

Carolyn looked at Sanson. "What did she say?"

Sanson shook his head. "She started crying and praising God and some other things I couldn't understand from her crying"

"She should have taken you up on your offer to give her a ride...I just hope she stays safe coming down here."

"I think she'll be alright. She's tough.. May not look it but she is as tough as they come."

Angela arrived just a few minutes before Pastor Dave. She flew past Randy at t he front door as h pointed down the hall to Angel's bed room. Her sudden cry of relief woke Angel up. For a moment, he seemed dazed and then embraced Angela as she fell sobbing on the bed beside him. Angel stared at Kelly and Randy for a moment and then smiled.

"What'cha doing, Pops?" Were his first words as he held out a hand to Randy who stood by Angel's bed, tears streaming down his cheeks.

Some what confused and dumbfounded, Angel struggled to sit up with Angela still embracing him, reluctant to let loose of her son. He kissed her on her cheek and then smiled as Sanson came in the room with Pastor Dave and Carolyn. "Wow." Is all he said as Pastor Dave clasped Angel's hands in both of his own, eyes closed and llps moving in a silent prayer. Angel looked around his room. "Am I home? Really?"

Kelly started to answer but choked up on more tears. Sanson nodded, grinning. "Welcome home, Mijo"

Releasing Pastor Dave's grip, Angel looked up at the ceiling, his eyes focused on something far beyond the sheet rock and shingles. "....They promised me...they..." He stopped and looked back at everyone in the room. "Oh...I have so many things to share with you all...so many, many things...you may not believe they're true but they are..."

Kelly found his voice. "You get some rest, Mijo...you can tell us later. We'll all be here."

Angel laid back down on his bed, smiling. "I love you all...so much..." He closed his eyes and almost immediately fell back asleep, still smiling.

Pastor Dave held out his hands to everyone and then bowed his head as everyone the circle around and over Angel's bed. Pastor

Dave waited for a moment and then began, "Thank you Lord God and Son Jesus for returning our 'mashed potatoes" the way we want him to be...."

Everyone was smiling and crying their own thanks when Pastor Dave finished his quiet, soulful prayer.

Everyone was at Kelly's big country kitchen table when Angel strode into the room a little past ten, sniffing the breakfast odors hanging in the air, and smiling. He walked around the table and stood behind the chairs where Caleb and Antonio were sitting. Placing his hands on their shoulders, he looked at Carolyn. "These look like your boys? They look like you. I'm Angel"

Carolyn stood up and walked around the table to Angel and held out her hand. "I'm Carolyn Rush and these are my sons. Caleb and Antonio. I'm a friend of Sheriff Sanson...and a reporter for CNN. That's how we met...when you were abducted. We're all so glad to have you back home "

Angel's head bobbed and he grinned. "Well I think when I'm through sharing with all of you what I've learned, I'm sure the word abduction will be replaced with 'chosen'".

Angela let out a little squeaky sound of happiness. "I told you...I told you!"

At a little past eleven thirty, they could hear the sounds of a helicopter circling the house and then landing in a field on the far side of the garden and chicken house. Carolyn asked her boys to go and help Irv and Mac bring in her supplies. By noon, they were up and running and Carolyn was interfacing with an ecstatic Sue and her CNN crew in the city preparing for an exclusive on the return of Angel, the young man who was abducted by the monstrous spaceship and feared dead because of the crushing forces of acceleration.

The stage was set in Kelly's living room with Angel and his mother on one side and Kelly and Randy of the other side. Sanson stood off to the side in the arch leading into the kitchen. Irv and Mac were on the left side by the bay window while Caleb and Antonio were on the opposite of the window. Both of Caroyln's boys were wide eyed, overwhelmed by events they had only seen on TV. Carolyn was about to begin when the sound of more helicopters interrupted them. Caleb and Antonio pointed out the window. "Some people are getting out of ambulances and their all dressed in those white infection suits except two guys in black suites. They're coming up to the door now." Antonio looked at Sanson who had moved to the front door just as they all heard the knocking.

"Keep filming!" Carolyn whispered to Irv and Mac just before Sanson opened the door, blocking the two men trying to enter. He pushed the most persistent man back so hard he almost went down the steps.

"What do you want?" Sanson barked and two men in hazmat suits came up the steps, stopping on the porch to see a red Cadillac SUV pull up behind the white ambulance. Looking at the two men, one tall and portly and the other short and slight of build, he had no doubt he was looking at the nameless Colonel and the offensive Major Borgis. When the larger man spoke, he no longer had any doubt.

"We understand the young man who was abducted has returned." The colonel said in a crisp tone.

"And what makes you think that? Sanson asked.

"Your County Supervisor called and said someone he knows at the casino where the young man's mother works told him she left work in a hurry because her son had returned although I think the word he used was "escaped."

Sanson glared past the men on the porch down to Carolton McMillan standing beside his shiny red Cadillac parked behind an ambulance where four armed men waited.

Carolton McMillan yelled up at Sanson. "Don't blame me for this! I just did my patriotic duty! That little pervert is contagious with God knows what from where's he's been with the devil's spawn!"

Sanson closed his eyes for a moment and bit his lip to keep from responding. He turned to the Colonel for a better explanation.

Inside his hazmat suit, the Colonel nodded that McMillan was right. "He's been exposed to unknown elements," He said in an authoritative tone, nodding toward Angel sitting between Kelly and his mother. "...and you all are now under a fourteen-day quarantine... but he has to come with us for an in-depth evaluation at a military hospital."Kelly lurched to his feet. "And where would that be and for how long?"

The Colonel shrugged. I'm not a doctor so I can't give you a time frame and as to where I'm not at liberty to say. I think you all know we're dealing with some very classified information here. Nothing like this has ever happened before and Angel is at the very center of it all...and...

Kelly interrupted the Colonel. "Can he call or write?"

The Colonel looked at Major Borgis for an answer." Major Borgis will oversee the program." As Major Borgis cleared his throat letting his squeaky voice ring true. His reply was terse as Sanson shot a dubious glance at Kelly. "I don't see a problem with that...but we need to leave now. The longer you are all exposed the greater the risk you'll all have to be hospitalized...not just quarantined. If any of you start to feel like you've been infected with something, call my number on this notice here." He handed a pink notice to Sanson and then motioned for the two men with him to suit Angel up. Angel smiled reassuringly, first to his mother and Kelly and then, with a nod to Sanson, and Carolyn Rush and her boys followed by another nod to Randy, and Pastor Dave. With his hood in place, his face disappeared behind the darkened face plexiglass but those in the room could hear him reassure them. "Don't worry. I'll be fine." Then, with a parting wave, he let the men lead him outside. There, as the rear door to the ambulance opened, Angel seemed to hesitate, and It was then that Major Borgis exposed his real nature by giving Angel a vicious shove from behind sending him sprawling to the floor of the vehicle. In an instant, Sanson leaped off the porch and headed toward the Borgis only to be stopped by a warning shot from one of the soldiers.

"You son of a....!" Sanson started to yell but caught himself as Borgis pulled his helmet off and flashed Sanson an insolent smile before stepping inside the ambulance. Still angry, Sanson and Kelly followed the ambulance to the small Columbia Airport and, with camera's on, monitored Angel's safe and uneventful transfer to the Army copter. As it rose up in the air, it suddenly swooped purposely and dangerously low over the sheriff's cruiser to where the prop wash kicked up stones and gravel against the vehicle, Sanson's fingers pressed against his chest and found his crucifix. Feeling it, he closed his eyes and said a prayer for Angel.

From the relatively short flight time of the helicopter of less than an hour, Angel estimated the hospital was somewhere close to Sacramento but being shrouded in his hazmat suit, complete with a hood covering, he was unsure especially when the gurney he was strapped to was wheeled across the hot tarmac a short distance and lifted into another plane. In minutes, he heard the whine of jet engines come to life and felt the plane's acceleration until it became airborne, and every sensation was gone except the muted roar or the engines. He tried asking whoever was with him where

Mr. B

they were going but was met with silence. Then the previous events of the day overcame him, and he fell fast asleep thinking about his mother, Pops, Boss and his lady friend from CNN, and Randy and Pastor Dave...and especially his "new friends' who had been so reassuring. He awakened hours later but only when he felt the jet's bump landing and became aware of his deplaning and being wheeled inside a building where, in total darkness, he was unstrapped from the gurney and rather roughly lifted and assisted into a chair. His head his head shroud was removed but still Angel could not see in the still total darkness. Then, after a few tense moments, came a man's voice from somewhere behind him in the blackness.

"Angel Torres...I presume?" It asked, quite calmly.

Angel cleared his throat and found himself nodding as he answered. "Yes, Sir...and who are you? He turned to see who It might be, but the darkness kept its secret.

"You may call me 'Twelve', Angel". It answered.

Angel found the man's response amusing. "Hey, how about letting me talk to number One?" Angel countered and heard a murmuring of chuckling behind him.

The voice of number Twelve continued unamused. "In time, Angel...in time. Do you have any idea of where you are?"

Angel shrugged in the darkness. "Not really. Maybe an airport of some kind...it smells a bit like my Pop's garage...welding smoke and stuff."

"Would you like to see?"

Again, Angel found himself nodding again. "Sure...of course."

In an instant, brilliant light flooded the cavernous room. But the room was filled to capacity with what looked like an enormous submarine, at least a thousand feet in length and three hundred feet high. Number Twelve's voice was soft, almost velvety. "This is the USS Pegasus...our nation's answer to the crisis all humanity is facing, Angel.. You're aware of this crisis....through your 'friends' right? Be honest with us, Angel."

Angel pivoted in his chair, turning to face Number Twelve and, nodding for the first time, saw the eleven other men sitting with him, all in dark suits with ties and white shirts, in two rows of six, their faces all impassive. Angel found himself smiling in recognition of them but he saw no response from any of them except two sitting together on the left side who deftly managed slight nods. Angel managed another slight smile in their direction.

Number Twelve went on. "She has the capacity for almost six thousand of the best and brightest minds in every discipline...all leaders and experts in their fields...which is why we are in hopes to form a partnership with 'your friends" to assure humanities best chances for a successful survival."

Angel sat quietly, listening to Number Twelve continue his presentation until finally he stopped, holding out his hand for Angel to speak. At first Angel didn't know where to start because he already knew what his answer would have to be and so, to preface his answer he decided to ask questions which he hoped would lead them to understanding what his answer would have to be. "Tell me...how many government officials are to be included in the total you'll be saving?"

Number Twelve hesitated and looked at his companions seated around him before he replied. "I don't have a precise figure on the breakdown." He replied, shifting uncomfortably in his chair.

Angel nodded, hesitating before continuing. "How about military?"

Number Twelve stared impassively at Angel but made no response so Angel continued, taking in a deep breath before letting his gaze drift over the group. " I count twelve of you...are you the remnants of the 'original majestic twelve' from the fifties? And are you and your families and friends included in who's to be saved?"

Finally. number twelve spoke up but did not answer Angel' question. "Where are you going with this, Mr. Torres?"

Angel managed to smile as he shook his head in disappointment. "I haven't quite finished my questions....I was about to ask how many Muslims, Jews, Taoists. Hindus. Taoists and other people of major or minus faiths are included?"

Number Twelve leaned back in his chair and stared coldly at Angel. "We didn't question their faith, Mr. Torres, Like this great country, their faith is of their choosing."

Angel agreed. "I know...I understand...but 'my friends' placed the quality of the person's soul first as the criteria for selection. Do you know your soul? Do you know that at birth, we are given bodies, brains, and souls and while the first two are lost at death, the soul is left to be judged...and it's judged by how much goodness is in it at the time of death. Little to no goodness and there is no salvation. How do my friends tell how much goodness is in our souls? I don't know...but they tell me they can tell who has the necessary goodness and who doesn't and that's what I go by...and two of you sitting here will pass...but the rest of you had better stick with the Pegasus here."

A voice spoke up from the darkness lingering in the far right and then a figure stepped out from the shadows. The somewhat squeaky voice was familiar to Angel and he quickly recognized Major Borgis who strutted into the space between Number Twelve and Angel. With his back to Angel. Borgis gestured to Angel behind him by pointing to him with his thumb over his shoulder.

"Don't be fooled by this petty boy...just take a good long look! I was told on good authority by his county supervisor that he's a registered pervert...he was arrested trying to sodomize another boy. It's all in their county records! So I guess 'goodness' is a relative quality to 'his friends. He laughed, while smirking at the same time. Borgis spun around to face Angel. "You're wasting your time if you think this holier-than-thou and "friends" are going to help us. If you ain't a believer, you're out...ain't that right...'Angel?" Borgis made the sound of Angel's name reek with ridicule.

For a moment, Angel hesitated but he realized he would have to admit the truth. He looked at the group in front of him. "My friends would do what God will do to any of us who die with barren souls. You cannot be saved"…but he stopped as Borgis drew his pistol and pointed it at Angel.

NumberTwelve stood up as if to intervene in some way but stopped as Borgis made a squeaky sound and dropped his pistol in an instant before his total body was consumed in flames, twisting and writhing as if made of flammable crepe paper. In seconds he was gone. The members or Majestic Twelve stared in horror first at the still swirling ashes and then at Angel sitting there in front of them, his eyes closed, just before the entire cavernous room plunged into darkness.

Number Twelve shouted. "Nobody move! He can' t get out. Get the lights back on! And shoot on sight."

It was late the following afternoon when Randy was making a second run picking up the chicken eggs in the hen house that he spotted Angel, still dressed in his now headless white hazmat suit walking down the field past the orchard by a row of grape vines toward the house. With a whooping cry, he set his tray of eggs down and raced to greet him. They embraced joyfully for a moment with Randy letting out a yell of happiness, pulling Angel into a trot toward the house and garage/

Kelly was stunned when the two young men walked into his shop. For a moment he simply stood in disbelief by his drill press before he broke into a lurching run, grabbing both young men in his powerful embrace. "How in the name of Heaven did you get here!?" He exclaimed, trying not to cry.

Mr. B

Angel shook his head in disbelief while tears of joy ran down his cheeks into almost two days growth of beard. "They were going to kill me, Pops....Borgis....Borgis...he burst into flames...he pulled his pistol on me and was going to shoot me and then he just burned up right in front of me...in seconds. It was bad...real bad! They thought I did it. And then the whole room went dark and this guy who was questioning me yelled for them to shoot me on sight...I guess I passed out because that's all I remember until our friends woke me up and let me out up on the hill...."

Kelly patted Angel on his back to comfort him And then gave him an extra hug for comfort. "I'm gonna call Boss. Mijo. You tell him everything when he gets here...and his lady friend too. Maybe she can put it on TV too. But come inside now and get some rest."

Sanson and Carolyn Rush and her two boys arrived at Kelly's house a few minutes past six with almost three hours of sunlight left in the day. Pastor Dave arrived almost fifteen minutes later but rather come inside, he stood in the parking area, talking and gesturing, obviously in prayer as Carolyn watched from the front window of the house. She looked over at Sanson and shook her head. "He doesn't talk much, does he?" She almost whispered. Sanson came over to join her. For a moment he watched Pastor Dave and then offered, "No, he doesn't...but when he does, you'd best be listening. He's the wisest man I know."

"How old is he?"

Sanson shrugged. "I don't know and to tell you the truth I never asked. According to Kelly, he was found when he was about five years old. I wasn't here at the time. At first everyone thought he was just a lost boy and that he got separated from some camping parents up around Twain Hart, but no one ever came in to claim him. Just as well...'cuz' he was covered with burn marks and a pentagram scar on his chest that looked like someone bent and heated a wire coat hanger. He must have gone through hell. He didn't talk and he went into foster care because no one would adopt him until Hazel and

Bert Cummings adopted him about a year later. They were older. They're gone now but they say they never missed a day of church... and home schooled him until the sixth grade. They passed when he was about nineteen and, in their will, they specified that all of their property be sold and the money to go to Dave for any seminary he chose. He chose not to go and instead he donated his inheritance to the county's foster care program and worked at a lumber yard. When the pastor at the local church retired, he applied and, from all that I heard, after the interviews, It was no contest. He was not only the best choice but the absolute most marvelous choice. They joked that he knew the Bible better than the authors. We're blessed to have him. Angel dotes on his every word...and I guess I do too. Maybe, if you'd like, you can go with me to next Sunday's service?"

Carolyn nodded. "I'd like that...and the boys too." She said and then watched as Pastor Dave finished his prayer with a solemn bow first to the west and the descending sun and then to the east where if would rise in the morning. And then, as if in perfect timing, Carolyn reached out and grabbed Sanson's arm for support as a tremor swept through Kelly's house, rattling pictures on the wall and setting the living room's two hanging lamp and fan chains to swinging.

Sanson shook his head. "That's the third one today." He said as Pastor Dave let himself in, a soft smile toward Carolyn's two boys on the couch and then hugs for Sanson and Carolyn. He looked around the room just as Kelly came in from down the hallway.

"Angel will be out in a minute...he's just finishing showering. Go ahead and sit down. Anyone want some lemonade? It's fresh. Just made it. Nice and cold."

Everyone accepted and Kelly was still in the kitchen when the freshly shaved Angel came in from the hallway followed by Randy. Hugs were exchanged followed by Angel announcing, " I've got a lot to tell you guys...you're not going to believe it.." Angel looked at Kelly coming in from the kitchen with a tray of glasses and a very

Mr. B

large pitcher of lemonade. Kelly set it down on the coffee table and said with a broad smile, "Welcome home…again…Mijo!"

Carolyn took it on herself to pour the lemonade, offering the first glass to Pastor

Dave and the second to Angel. The third went to Sanson who lifted it to Angel.

`"So what's new, Mijo?" He asked, smiling ."

Shaking his head and returning Sanson's smile. Angel sank down in the easy chair to the left, flanking the fireplace. "It's unbelievable, Boss….they actually were going to kill me…or at least try to. I guess when I started to tell them that our friends would not help them… they called it a partnership…and that I knew their secret…I mean it was right there in front of me…this huge spaceship that looked like a giant submarine. They said it was their humanitarian effort to save about six thousand of what they called their best and brightest which turned out to be almost half government and half military with the balance technical experts…kind of like the Titanic…the rich go first. Our friends saved me…just like they promised but just how I don't know. But where's my mom? Angel asked.

"We're picking her up. I made reservations at Jimmy's to welcome you back, Mijo, and she wanted some time to look good for you."

Carolyn giggled. "How much time does 'perfection' take? She looks better than the old Dolly Parton in her prime.'

Sanson laughed , "Coming from someone who looks better than an old Grace Kelly in her prime is a nice compliment!"

Carolyn laughed again. "I'll take that!" She said, standing on her toes to give Sanson a kiss on his cheek and then turning to wink at her boys.

Jimmy'a Chimys was busy with the dinner crowd. Sanson and Kelly took advantage of the sheriff's parking lot across the street and walked across Washington from the old courthouse. When they entered, it was like a political reunion with almost everyone greeting Sanson's party almost like favored candidates, especially Carolyn and Sanson with Angel receiving welcoming hugs from those who had learned of his ordeal. Jimmy was still there and he quickly set up two tables for ten against the back wall where Sanson was able to survey everyone coming in the front door. It was an old accommodation given to sheriff and police ever since a deranged gunman had come in the front door and opened fire, killing the old city police chief and wounding two other officers some thirty plus years ago. And it was from that vantage point that Carolyn first spotted the two men in black standing outside and just to the left in the front windows. She elbowed Sanson and whispered, "Outside…to the left."

Sanson grunted and paused a moment before casually letting his eyes focus on Carolyn's warning. He patted her arm in thanks. "Looks like the scouts are here already." He said in a low voice and staring hard just as Elliot, in uniform, came in the door with his wife, Dottie and young son, Junior. Elliot gave Sanson a wave and headed through the crowd to the back tables. When his wife saw what was happening, she made a sour face at her husband which quickly became a Cheshire grin when she saw the encounter could not be avoided. A pretty but not a beautiful woman, her pose became rigid as she was introduced to Carolyn with her only fawning comment being, "I've seen you on TV." This was followed by a brief nod and brittle smile to Angelica and a terse. "I've seen you at the casino…" while Elliot made the rounds shaking hands, first with Pastor Dave, and then everyone else with the last being Sanson who motioned him to come closer as Junior, following his father's example, started shaking hands until he reached across the table to shake Angel's hand who stood halfway up to accommodate the boy until his mother reached out and hooked a finger in the collar of his shirt and pulled him back.

Mr. B

"That's enough!" She snapped until Elliot intervened and nodded for his son to shake Angel's hand while he scowled at his wife who abruptly turned away and moved swiftly towards the front door where she stopped, waiting. A pall of silence hung over the table until Elliot somewhat apologized.

"Sorry about that...she listens to her father too much." He said quietly and then looked in the direction where Sanson was pointing.

"Hey, Amigo...there are two men dressed all in black right out in front. If they come in, can you intercept them for me and get them to leave? I'm sure they're after Angel here.... We just want to enjoy a nice welcome home dinner." Elliot leaned closer to Sanson and whispered but everyone could hear him. "How many times do you want me to shoot them?

Sanson couldn't hide his grin. "I don't care as long as it's in self-defense. " He said and then added, " Why don't you come by Kelly's house after dinner and hear what Angel has to share?"

Elliot nodded. 'Can I bring Junior with me after I drop Dottie off?"

"Sure...but she's welcome to come too if she wants."

Elliot grimaced. "Yeah...sure."

It was almost nine and almost dark when the small caravan Sanson was leading pulled up in front of Kelly's house where Elliot and junior were already waiting. As soon as they reached the front porch Kelly announced, "They've been here so I'm sure they've planted something."

Sanson looked around, puzzled how Kelly could tell. Kelly smiled. "The little piece of candle wax in the door lock Is gone. They looked for everything but that, so you might want to look around when we go in..."

Sanson nodded, impressed, as he stepped inside as Kelly announced, "If you've got leftovers there's room in the fridge." He went into the kitchen while the others sank contentedly in the chairs and on the couch and waited for Kelly to return. When he did a few moments later, all eyes turned on Angel who stood behind his mother's chair.

Angel's brown eyes scanned the room. "I hope you all will listen and believe what I'm going to tell you…but it's all true…and it's all going to happen."

Carolyn held up her right hand like a student in a class. "Angel? Can I record this on my phone? I want to send it to the office."

Angel smiled. "Absolutely…No problem…but what I'm going to share goes way, way back to a teacher who lived and taught on the southern tip of Argentina. He was an amateur astronomer and one night way back in the thirties, he saw something that puzzled him. He didn't know it at the time but it was a Black Hole, way, way off. He reported it to his astronomer club buddies and no one really paid attention to it at first until he and his whole family disappeared one day. He didn't show up for school and when they went to investigate, they found his house had burned to the ground…but no bodies. A couple of years later, the Black Hole was discovered again but no one had the skill or the interest to figure out its trajectory so again it was just forgotten. But later as the science of math became more refined, they discovered the thing was going to swing through our solar system or at least close to it…and it was then it was decided to keep it a secret to avoid public panic. Now that brings us to now and our friends who are going to help us. You see, way, way back in the past, a similar thing was going to happen about a hundred and fifty million years ago when a huge asteroid's trajectory was going to hit Earth and the beings by the name of the Ciruleans could see what was going to happen, Now, they weren't as advanced as our friends and they didn't have the science to alter its path but they were able to see that there were some life forms that were worth saving…notably our friends. And they did just that and resettled them on another planet. Now, in the hundred and fifty million years since then, our friends, our saviors, made a solemn vow to develop the science to make sure that no random acts in our solar system or galaxy would ever destroy promising signs of life. And that's where we are today... Believe it or not, focus on the wall by the front door but, I'm warning you, you are going to see the terrifying prospectus of what's going to happen when the Black Hole is going to be closest to the Earth in three months from now but on the far side of the sun. We can already feel the small earthquakes. Watch! Venus, with its orbit closest to the Black Hole, it will be gone, sucked like sticky gum into or, better told, pushed and stretched by gravity into the grips of the Black Hole which science now believes is a giant wormhole into another dimension with less gravitational force than what we have on this side. Ou gravity is being sucked into the other side Earth is more fortunate. Our orbit will place us almost opposite of Venus's orbit and furthest away...but watch now what the Black Hole does to the sun. You see? Huge amounts of hydrogen will be sucked out of our sun. Mercury, on the far side, will be sucked into the sun itself...and our Earth will now go through the agony of immense distortion through hellish fires, eruptions, earthquakes, floods and avalanches. Watch this... The polar ice caps will melt in a matter of hours and the oceans and seas will rise and form inland seas that rush into all the low lying areas from Louisiana up into Illinois, joining the Great Lakes. Middle America will be a gigantic sea. Florida will disappear under the rising Atlantic. The islands of Cuba, Puerto Rico, Haiti and their neighbors will be gone too, and the Panama Canal will be under water from the Atlantic to the Pacific. The Atlantic will rise up against the East Coast mountain ranges and only the tips of the tallest building along every coastline will be visible above water. Connecticut and Rhode Island will be gone ...no more, submerged like their other low-lying neighbors, The same for the Netherlands. Their dikes will be useless and for the people along the Mediterranean coast line it will be the same. Those living in the mountain areas will suffer as well from earthquakes and landslides but they will be the most fortunate. The rest of the world? Indonesia? Australia, Japan? China? Alaska? Angel stopped and studied the expression on the faces which ranged from disbelief to horrified to terrified. Randy seemed to be handling it best when he asked, "What about Yellowstone?

Angel grimaced and bit his lip. "That's the biggest worry for our friends. I mean when it blows, we all need to be out of here. It will take just about everything out."

Junior, Elliot's son, raised his hand as if he was in school. Wide eyed in wonder, he spoke quietly, "I've been to Yellowstone. It's pretty. It has big, big fountains. Is this just a movie or is it real?"

Before Elliot spoke, he wrapped his son in his arms and tried to wipe the tears away in his own eyes. "Don't worry, good guy. You'll be safe! I'll explain it to you later, okay?"

Junior managed a small smile of trust.

Sanson changed the subject. "You remember Borgis claimed you were gonna be mashed potatoes if you flew as fast as they said. How'd you survive, Angel?"

Even Angel seemed relieved to change the subject. He managed a grin.. "Water...can you believe that?"

"Water? Sanson echoed, his expression, like the others, one of puzzlement.

"Yeah, water. When we studied hydraulics in school, they said water had some unique properties in that it could only expand and never shrink no matter how much pressure and heat were put on it. Well, they put me in a globe of water with air before they took off and since water can't be crushed, so to speak, neither can anything that's put into it...which was me in this case and the friends taking care of me. Simple but amazing. Another thing I learned.... gravity isn't 'pull', it's push. It's all around us...but it can vary in pressure, and it keeps everything from exploding from balloons to planets and suns... and Black Holes. When it's too weak, a sun will explode in a super nova. Another thing, one of the big dangers in space travel are gravity waves. They said they lost some ships to them before they learned to detect them. They're like those monster waves in the oceans that come out of nowhere on clear days when the ocean is calm. Hey, we've lost ships to them. It's amazing how much they know that's really simple when you stop to think about it. And you know who they are? Our friends? They're the raptors from the dinosaur days and the Ciruleans noticed how good they were to each other, especially family wise and tried to live what I guess you could call 'the good life. So, the ones they could save were taken to another planet. And there, they got better and better at being goof and made it their mission in life to help and rescue others who seemed to want the same kind of life…like us."

Sanson shook his head. "Raptors…I mean honest to God real raptors?"

Angel grinned. "Yep…but they've changed a bit in all the time that's passed, I mean a hundred and fifty million years, it's gotta happen…the old Darwin process."

"They're that old?" Carolyn asked, and in the darkness that had finally settled in, she stopped, noticing the bright lights of cars pulling up out in front followed by car doors slamming and barking voices and the sound of heavy boots running up the steps to the front door, slamming it open.

Two young faced men with menacing eyes burst in, leveling their fierce weapons in a sweeping motion at everyone in the room. Elliot, still in uniform, was the first to speak as two more armed men entered. He stood up, his voice fierce with anger. "Don't you be pointing your weapons at my son!" He barked, letting his hand go to his own pistol.

"At ease!" Another voice half yelled as a general strode into the room. The armed soldiers lowered their weapons, but their expressions remained fierce and threatening. The general eyes squinted and swept the room, fastening on Angel still standing behind his mother in front of the fireplace. "You! You come with me. I have a federal warrant for your arrest as an escaped prisoner also wanted for the murder of an Army officer." He turned to one of the armed men. "Cuff him!'

Sanson stood up, dominating the room. He shook his head and then faced the two men in black who had just entered the room and stood there, one or them smiling as if he had won. The man who had started forward tp cuff Angel, hesitated and looked doubtfully to the General who frowned at the young soldier's hesitation.

"I said cuff him!" the General barked.

Sanson interrupted before the soldier could comply. "Boy? I wouldn't do that if I were you. You could be struck dead…just like the Major you probably heard about. Why don't you let that smiling man in Black by the door do it? He seems to think this is all fun and games. No offense but this is not a boy's game…it's a man's game."

Sanson watched the man's smile flicker for a moment in doubt and then be replaced with a smirk and a 'why not' shrug when the Geneal turned to him. With the General's nod of approval, the man in black stepped forward and took the cuffs from the wide eyed and much relieved young soldier who closed his eyes in relief and then opened them when the man in Black made a grunting sound and slumped to the floor either unconscious or dead. The young soldier bolted for the front door, pushing past the second man in Black who made the mistake of drawing his gun, only to be immediately engulfed in flames as he lurched toward the porch just outside where a chorus of disbelieving shouts greeted the sight of his flaming body. When the stunned General turned back to Angel, his mouth fell open when he noticed Sanson was no longer in the room along with Carolyn and her two sons as well as Kelly, Angelica and Randy.

He stammered in shock. "Wh…where are…where did they go!" He demanded, looking around as if they might be hiding.

Angel smiled, knowingly. "They're with our friends…" He said quietly. "The second man in Black was intent on killing him…and our friends could not let him kill our leader."

"Your leader!?" The general repeated in confusion. "I...I thought you.."

Angel shook his head. "No...I'm just the messenger. Boss was chosen to lead us once we are all safe. Go outside and look up. You'll see an area where there are no stars...that's their ship....that's where Boss and his friends, my Pops, and my mother are right now...all probably just as confused as you are now."

The General seemed to dissolve in doubt. "I don't understand..." he began, and Pastor Dave interrupted him and faced him, sympathetically.

"You don't understand because you have no 'soul", sir. Or none to very little. You follow orders. John Sanson follows God...and Christ. When we're born, we are all given certain things...a body...a brain... and a 'soul". And we must choose which one we will serve. Some of us only serve our bodies...with excess of food and drink and drugs... while others serve the brain looking for power through greed and hate...and jealousy...through money and prestige...and then there are those who serve their souls first, trying to do as much good as possible. But of the three gifts we receive in life, only the soul moves on to the next life...and only if there is a record of doing good for yourself and others. If the soul of a person is empty, then there is no gift of a second life...none...only goodness earns it... I hate to say it but. goodness in your soul is like having money in the bank...but a hellish moment comes when a person realizes this is the truth and realizes he or she is truly broke with no claim to the reward of the next life. Their souls are empty. Then comes the true terror of hell in a moment of eternal regret. God cannot and will not change the sinner, only the sinner has the power and responsibility to do that by accepting the power of God and Christ. You, General, you know who you serve...your body?...with excess? Your brain?... through a desire for power and influence which you think brings you safety? Perhaps it does here...but it adds nothing to your soul. Angel's 'friends', our friends, know your soul just like the rest of us. How? I have no idea...

but they seem to have a way of looking into our souls...but you will find out...in an instant if you decide to try and kill Angel just like the men in Black or Borgis who were so confident and thought power here would protect them. Now, they are gone. Power here is nothing, temporary at best, unless it is for doing good. It's your life...and your choice only...so you and all of your men need to think long and hard about this for we are all born as privileged fools with the option to choose which path to take.

Something in the General seemed to waver and then disappear until another young soldier burst into the room forgetting to salute and blurted, "They.re gone, sir!"

"Who's gone?!" He demanded sharply.

"Three of my men! They were standing right there with us and I heard their weapons drop and I looked over and they were gone... just like in those old 'beam-me-up-Scottie movies on TV!"

"What the.....? The General started to say and then to the soldiers remaining in the room and he uttered a terse. "Out!" Then, wavering with a final moment of indecision he turned back to Pastor Dave and Angel with a quiet, "I'm sorry...and thank you." With that, he left.

Carolton McMillan could not and would not believe the report he received from the military that all of the 'perpetrators" had escaped through "unknown means" when attempts were made to apprehend them. He seethed with even greater fury as all of the contact numbers he had been given now came back as 'no longer in service" or put on 'please hold' with no one ever answering. To further frustrate him, the Sonora City Department of Street Repair and Maintenance called his office later the next night to report unauthorized overnight removal of properties, both private and public, from within the city's limits. Outraged that something like this could happen on his watch, he set out early the next morning as the sun was rising, he drove by to inspect the damage. He recognized the street as Sanson's street and when he drove by, he was astonished at seeing the whole property was gone, with the house and separate garage and the back yard's fruit trees all gone as if a giant surgical knife had come in and cleanly excised everything with unbelievable precision. His neighbor came out to share his own astonishment and reported that Sanson had come back the previous night to pick up his dog, Husky, and his cat, Woodpile and left with a cheerful, "God Bless!" But next properties showed even more of the same astonishing works. . Jimmy's Chimis had been a narrow brick edifice twenty-four foot wide sandwiched in between Carter's Drugstore and Sorenson's Shoes. Now it was gone. Totally, with not a brick damaged on either of the neighbors' buildings. Even more astonishing, McMillan stared in disbelief at the same disappearance of the old courthouse across Washington Street. Again, it looked like a precise removal of everything from sidewalks to trees to the parking lots behind. "My God!" He whispered to himself with a feeling akin to terror seizing him as he watched the early morning commuters slow down and stare in befuddlement at the unexplanable disappearances. A feeling of insecurity assailed him. Breathing hard, he called Sanson's number and received recording telling him that the party he was calling and not available and to please leave a message. McMillan decided that Sanson could be down at Kelly Walker's place in Jamestown. He called the emergency county number and asked for backup from the Sheriff's Department and Elliot Mitchell, his son- in- law, but was informed that Elliot could not be reached as he was still off duty and would not return until seven AM.

    McMillan glanced at his watch. It showed six fifteen with the sun now up. And now, close to complete panic, McMillan called and asked for the Sheriff's night commander to accompany him or meet him there since the area was beyond the scope of the Sonora Police Department. He felt his heart racing as he turned on Rabbit's

Run and sped down the narrow road. Braking to a screeching halt, he came to what used to be Kelly Walker's house and business. It was all gone. Everything. The house, the repair shop, the gas station, the garden, the hen house, the vineyard and orchard, the row upon row of bright marigold flowers all gone. Even the pond with the year-round spring was gone, its water shooting out the side of the cleanly carved hillside and dribbling across the road in front of him.

McMillan reached for his cell phone and, with shaking fingers, he dialed his son-in-law's private number just as a massive earthquake shook his car, and splitting the road with a giant six foot crevice in front of him.

McMillan screamed into his phone. "Elliot!
"ELLIOT!"

McMillan kept screaming.

"ELLIOT! You son of a…" His voice choked on tears.
'ELLIOT!"
"ELLIOT!"

The earth rumbled again, harder.